"What is it you want from me, Ms. Callie Stevens?"

"I don't really know you, Mr. Grant Carver, but I know your type."

"My type? Please enlighten me. What is my type?"

She tried to glare at him, but it didn't come off.

"Go on," he pressed. "I want to know what you think 'my type' is."

"Okay." She raised her chin. "Type A for arrogant. Type C for controlling. Type T for tyrant. Should I go on?"

"I get the picture. So sue me."

"I just might do that," she said. "And you know what? If I'd had the chance, I'm sure I *would* have fired you." And with that nonsensical statement of defiance, she turned and stormed off.

Callie was nagging at him like a burr under a saddle. He'd mulled it over and he'd come to a decision.

Callie Stevens was the perfect woman to have his baby.

Dear Reader,

I'm so glad you've decided to try my book. I hope you enjoy it.

My editor suggested readers might be interested in gardening tips related to the story. At first I wasn't sure I could pull that off. Callie Stevens does begin her romance with Grant Carver because her orchid plant knocks him to the floor, so the relevance is there. But my main experience in growing orchids has usually been to buy one at the nursery, bring it home and watch it slowly die. It's always so sad as those gorgeous blooms begin to shrivel up. The big, strappy leaves left behind seem so reproachful. And I never know what I'm doing wrong.

But last year a miracle happened. I put two such remnant pots into the garden window over my kitchen sink and just left them there. Now and then I would pour in a little water. It was pure laziness that kept me from dumping them in the trash. And then one day I noticed a strange, probing sort of stalk growing out of one, and then the same from the other. And suddenly, blooms burst out. They didn't look quite like the ones that had been there before—a little more generic, I think. But they were lovely and lasted weeks. So that's my gardening tip. Put your spent orchid in indirect northeast light from a window over your kitchen sink. (Does the moisture help? Who knows?) And wait for a miracle.

In the meantime, happy reading!

All the best,

Raye Morgan

RAYE MORGAN
The Boss's Pregnancy Proposal

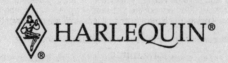

TORONTO • NEW YORK • LONDON
AMSTERDAM • PARIS • SYDNEY • HAMBURG
STOCKHOLM • ATHENS • TOKYO • MILAN • MADRID
PRAGUE • WARSAW • BUDAPEST • AUCKLAND

ISBN-13: 978-0-373-03934-0
ISBN-10: 0-373-03934-4

THE BOSS'S PREGNANCY PROPOSAL

First North American Publication 2007.

This edition published by arrangement with Harlequin Books S.A.

® and TM are trademarks of the publisher. Trademarks indicated with ® are registered in the United States Patent and Trademark Office, the Canadian Trade Marks Office and in other countries.

www.eHarlequin.com

Printed in U.S.A.

Raye Morgan has been writing romances for years and has been fostering romance in her own family at the same time (current score: two boys married, two more to go). Raye has published over seventy romances, and claims to have many more waiting in the wings. She still lives in Southern California with her husband and whichever son happens to be staying at home at the moment. When not writing, she can be found feverishly working on family genealogy and scrapbooking. So many pictures, so little time!

Don't miss Raye's next fantastic book:
Bride by Royal Appointment
In The Royal House of Niroli continuity
In Harlequin Presents®—out soon!

To Patience—
for her compassion, perseverance,
and…well, patience!
Thanks so much.

CHAPTER ONE

EMPTY offices were dark and spooky at night.

Callie Stevens took the stairs. She didn't want to use the elevator. Too noisy, and the last thing she wanted was to draw any attention from the night watchman.

By the time she'd climbed to the fifth floor of ACW Properties, she was beginning to rethink that position. But she had to be careful. After all, she'd just been fired by Harry Carver, the elderly CEO. She wasn't supposed to be here at all.

Reaching the sixth-floor landing, she stopped to catch her breath and listen for signs of life. Glass sconces lined the hallways giving off a dim light, but nothing was stirring. A sigh of relief and she made her way toward the area where her little cubicle stood among all the rest.

The light from the hallway cast an eerie spell over the room, lengthening shadows and making hiding places where they weren't meant to be. She stopped for a moment, orienting herself and feeling a sharp pang of regret. She'd liked this job. She was going to miss it—and the money that went with it.

Looking around quickly, she finally saw the object of her quest—her treasured orchid plant. She'd left it behind during the hectic ten minutes they'd given her to clean out her desk before escorting her off the premises. She'd been afraid someone might have thrown it in the trash, but there it was up on the high corner of a metal bookcase.

She glanced around quickly for something to climb on. There was no stepladder, so she pushed a chair over and hopped up, stretching high. Her fingers could barely reach. She'd just made contact with the ceramic pot that held her floral darling when the lights of the room snapped on and a deep male voice sent a shock wave slicing through her.

"Looking for something, Ms. Stevens?"

She screamed.

It wasn't a very loud scream, more of a yelp, really. But it was enough to cause her to lose her balance. She grabbed at the edge of the shelf, but it was too late. She was falling and so was the ceramic pot with the orchid she'd come back to rescue.

She hit bottom with a thud, but not the sharp, painful smack she'd expected. It took a couple of seconds for her adrenaline to fade and her mind to register that the man who'd startled her had stepped forward and tried to break her fall, and that she'd smashed him to the floor for his trouble—and now they were locked together in an embarrassing tangle of hair and limbs.

This was not good.

"Oh!"

She scrambled to her feet and looked down at him. It was Grant Carver—her ex-supervisor—nephew of the CEO who'd fired her and just about the last person she wanted to see.

He looked a bit dazed. She could probably make a run for it and get away. She drew in a sharp breath, wondering....

But then she saw the ooze of blood at the corner of his mouth and she gasped. The back of her head must have hit him in the face.

"Oh!" she cried again, dropping to her knees beside him. "Are you all right? Oh my God, you're hurt."

His deep blue eyes opened and regarded her coolly from beneath thick, dark lashes. "Ya think?" he murmured. Grimacing, he reached up to touch his lip and drew back a bloody hand.

"Oh, I'm so sorry," she said. "What can I do?"

"Here's what you can do," he said, his voice husky. "You can walk over to that desk." He gestured toward the supervisor's desk.

She jumped up and did as he suggested, looking back at him questioningly. "This one?"

"Yes." He nodded, and winced in a way that made her bite her lip in regret. "Now you can pick up that phone."

She did so, still watching him for directions.

"And you can dial 9 for building security. Tell them to call the police. We've got an intruder who needs arresting."

"Oh!" She slammed the phone back down.

She should have known. All her compassion drained away. She'd worked with Grant Carver quite a few times in the year and a half she'd been here and she had yet to figure him out. Though he was cool and somewhat sardonic on the surface, she'd often sensed an underlying current in him that disturbed her. The man had secret demons.

Most of her female co-workers tended to swoon as he passed, but she'd never been one to fall for wide shoulders and crystal-blue eyes. She knew from experience that male beauty could hide a shriveled soul.

Still, did it matter? She didn't really believe he would have her arrested. Tongue-lashed, certainly. But arrested? No.

"Sorry to disappoint you," she said, walking slowly back to stand with hands on her hips over where he'd pulled himself up into a sitting position on the floor.

He was rubbing the back of his dark head as though he'd hit it hard enough to get a lump. He was still dressed in suit pants and a white shirt, though that was open at the neck and his tie and suit coat were missing. She couldn't ignore the fact that he was a very large, very handsome man. But that hadn't mattered when she'd worked for him. Why should it matter now?

"You're not going to have me arrested," she told him firmly, watching as he pulled a handkerchief from his pocket and held it to his cut lip.

He looked skeptical. "I'm not?"

She shook her head. "No, you're not."

"I don't know," he said doubtfully, looking up at her. He began counting off the charges on his fingers. "Trespassing. Possibly breaking and entering. Definitely assault and battery. Assault with a deadly…" He frowned. "What is that thing?"

She picked the remnants up off the floor. The purple glazed pot was in pieces, but the inner plastic container looked unharmed. It held a couple of leathery leaves and a long stalk with a full violet blossom wobbling giddily at the end of it.

"It *was* an orchid pot."

"Okay. Assault with an orchid pot."

He considered that for a moment, frowned slightly, then shook his head. "On second thought, maybe we ought to skip the phone call," he said, rising effortlessly to his feet and towering over her. "I can exact my own brand of punishment."

That gave her a momentary shiver, but she would rather eat dirt than let him see her squirm. She tried to tell herself that his height was partly exaggerated by the finely tooled cowboy boots he wore, but she knew the truth. He was tall.

"I hardly think that will be necessary," she said, holding his gaze with her own, no shivers showing.

"And I hardly think you're in the position to make these decisions," he shot back.

"Look, the only reason I fell was because you startled me." A thought occurred to her and she frowned. "What are you doing here, anyway?"

He stared at her. "What am *I* doing here? It's my family's company."

She shrugged. She wasn't going to give up any ground if she could help it. "I thought you were off in West Texas somewhere for the week."

"I'm back."

So it seemed. Just more of her bad luck. "It's after hours. This building is supposed to be empty."

He looked at her as though he'd decided she had a screw loose after all. "Oh, I see. So *I'm* the one not following rules."

Ridiculous. She knew that. But what the heck—the best defense was a good offense. She'd heard that many times. And she certainly had no intention of begging for mercy. So what else could she do?

"Exactly," she said, holding his gaze. "You're certainly the one who caused all the trouble."

He stared at her and suddenly, he grinned. And then he laughed.

She stepped back, startled again. Who knew he even had a sense of humor? She felt hesitant, thrown off guard. She was perfectly comfortable defending herself against a strong man, but she wasn't sure what to do with a man who laughed.

"Oh, I don't know," he drawled at last, eyes sparkling. "I say we blame it on the orchid. That makes about as much sense."

She looked down at what she'd gathered in her hands. Watching her, he held back a chuckle. She seemed to be taking him so seriously. And that reminded him of what he'd always liked about her. She wasn't a flirt.

He'd had his fill of flirts. Women sometimes seemed to respond to him like flowers opened to the sun. There'd been a time when he'd reveled in it. But that time had long since passed. Now it just got in the way.

Not that he was dead to physical appeal. With her thick blond hair and her large dark eyes, Callie Stevens was a looker and he had the same involuntary attraction to her any normal man would have. Still, he was experienced enough to know it didn't mean a thing. It would never touch him where he lived. Nothing much did anymore. Life was more tolerable that way.

"Orchids are plants," Callie was saying, looking at him with a crease between her brows that told him she knew he'd been teasing her, but wanted to challenge him anyway.

"Agreed. So what?"

She looked triumphant. "No free will. You can't assign blame to them. They have no choice in how they're flung about."

He had the grace to pretend chagrin. "I'll have to admit, you've got a point there," he said.

She hesitated only briefly. If he was admitting things, it was definitely time for her to make a grand departure.

"Of course I do," she said regally. "Now if you'll excuse me..."

She turned to go, but his hand on her arm brought her to a halt before she'd made a convincing attempt at a getaway. She looked up at him, wishing she could read the intentions in those clear blue eyes.

"Hold it," he was saying. "We're not finished here."

For the first time, she really did feel uneasy. She was alone in a darkened building with a man she really didn't know all that well. She'd been one with six others in the research group under Grant Carver, but they were only one of four groups he supervised. She had worked closely with him on a couple of projects, but there'd been a natural reserve between them and it hadn't only come from her end of the relationship.

She'd had a strange encounter with him once, months ago, where he'd made a proposal that was so off-the-wall, she sometimes wondered if she'd dreamed it. She'd turned him down and he hadn't seemed to hold it against her. But it had made her wonder about him. She knew there was tragedy in his life. If she hadn't known it from the office buzz, she would have recognized it in the depths of his eyes.

But that was all he'd ever revealed. In fact, she'd probably seen more honest emotion from him tonight than she'd seen in over a year of working for him.

For some reason, her attention dropped to his open shirt and stuck there for a beat too long. It wasn't as though she could actually see anything. The lighting cast dark shadows on his chest. But the fact that the crisp white fabric that was usually closed behind a tie now lay open, exposing something mysterious, was somehow intimate and exciting in a way she hadn't expected. Her pulse stuttered in surprise and began to race.

But she couldn't let him know.

"I'm finished," she responded, looking back up quickly. "I came for my orchid and I've got it."

"There must have been an easier way," he noted dryly.

"Probably," she said. "But I never seem to do things the easy way."

He nodded. "You do things in a pretty good way, from what I've seen. As I remember it, you worked on the Ames Ranch project last year, didn't you?"

Work. Yes, if he kept this on a professional level, she could handle it. If only he weren't touching her. His fingers had curled around her arm in a casual grip, but when she tried to pull away, he didn't budge. For all intents and purposes, he had her trapped.

"Yes, sir, I did," she said stoutly.

"And quite handily, too." His handsome head tilted as he studied her from narrowed eyes. "You were the only one on the staff who seemed to understand what the hell was going on most of the time."

You actually noticed? She didn't really say it, but it was on the tip of her tongue. But she would have followed that up with, *Why didn't you give me any credit for that at the time?*

He was gazing at her speculatively. "I think we could do some good work together. I've got a new project coming up…"

Her eyes widened. Tossing her thick blond hair back, she stared right into his deep eyes.

"Too late. Your uncle fired me today. Didn't you know?"

She'd expected him to react with surprise. Maybe even shock. After all, he'd just admitted she was one of the best employees he had. When he realized what had happened surely he would do something to straighten things out. Surely he would tell her he'd reprimand whomever it was that put her on the list for layoffs. Maybe he would invite her to come back and even give her a nice fat raise to make up for…

Her head jerked as she came out of her dream and heard how he actually responded to her announcement of her firing.

"Yes, I know."

"You know?" she echoed stupidly.

He knew. He'd probably put her on the list on purpose. *Hey, fire the blond chick—she's good but she gets on my nerves. Smart is one thing, smart aleck is another. Get rid of her.*

Suddenly she was furious—as angry as she'd been when she'd first heard she was a goner. Pulling away from his grip on her arm, she turned on him fiercely.

"But you think you know everything, don't you? Did you also know I just lost my second job, the one I use to help get out of a mountain of debt that's about to eat me alive? Did you also know that I'm about to be evicted from my apartment because I can't pay the rent?

Do you ever think about things like that when you casually toss people overboard? Or are we just like chess pieces in a big, careless game that doesn't mean a thing to you?"

His handsome face could have been cut from stone. "Are you finished?"

"No! There are others just like me. Everyone in the research department, in fact. We were all living by the skin of our teeth, paycheck to paycheck…because you don't exactly pay a lot to your lower-level employees, do you? And now every one of us is out on her ear, wondering where the next meal is coming from…."

"Okay, enough," he demanded, stopping the words in her throat. "Can the outrage, Norma Rae. We don't encourage peasant rebellions around here." He'd pulled out another handkerchief and was wiping at the blood on his face and dabbing at the mess it had made on the front of his shirt.

"Imagine the damage you could have done with a pitchfork," he muttered.

A sharp retort sprang to her lips, but before she could get the words out, she noticed that the bleeding was worse than she'd thought. She had to bite her lip to hold back a small cry. Every instinct in her wanted to leap forward and do something about the wound. Heal him. Maybe even comfort him. After all, it was pretty much her fault, no matter what she said to him.

The funny thing was he'd never looked more attractive to her. His dark hair was mussed, some of it falling down over his forehead. And there was a sort of vulnerability to him because of the cut and the blood and all. He usually looked so invincible. It was a refreshing change in a way.

And then he ruined it all by looking up with his mouth twisted in the usual sardonic style.

"Come along, my little attempted murderess," he said, turning toward the corridor. "You're going to have to fix what you've broken."

She followed willingly enough as he led the way to his office. Guilt was making her pliable for the moment.

She hadn't been in his office very often. She knew women who looked for any excuse to make a visit here, but she wasn't one of them. As the best-looking unattached male—and the CEO's nephew—he was considered quite a catch.

She'd never found him all that attractive herself. Too much arrogance there. That take-charge attitude did nothing but put her off. It reminded her too much of her short but miserable marriage. Not that Grant was anything like Ralph, really. At least Grant's arrogance was based on a certain level of competence. Ralph's had been mostly bluster.

Still, she'd vowed she would never again let a man rule her life the way her husband had tried to rule hers all those years and she tended to stay clear of men like Grant.

His office was a lot like him—handsome and well-maintained. Plush carpeting muffled sound; leather, wood and black glass provided a rich atmosphere. One framed photograph, set high at the back of the office, immediately drew the eye. The beautiful dark-haired woman holding an even more beautiful dark-eyed toddler had to be the wife and child she knew had died in a horrible car accident a few years ago.

The tragedy of losing a child—she could hardly bear to think of it. They said he'd changed after the accident. That he became a completely different person. She had no way of knowing what he'd been like before, but she found it hard to believe he'd been full of joy and laughter and the milk of human kindness in his earlier incarnation. The man she knew was totally focused on business and success and not much else.

So…just as she was a widow, he was a widower. She'd never put those two identities together like that before. Just the thought made her jump back mentally, as though she'd put her hand on a hot stove. No, she didn't want to go there.

"So, where is your first-aid kit?" she asked. She put the pieces of her orchid pot on the desk and turned, noting there was a door leading to a private bathroom.

"I'll take care of the cut," he said, beginning to shrug out of his shirt. "You take care of the bloodstains on this."

He held out the shirt to her but she had a hard time noticing. Her attention was caught and held by the incredible sight of his beautiful torso.

Men his age weren't supposed to look this good. He had to be in his thirties. By then, most males she knew had started to let lust for potato chips and beer overcome the desire to work out at the gym. Somebody had forgotten to clue Grant in to the routine. He was as gorgeous as a Greek statue.

And just as cold, she reminded herself quickly, working hard to keep her breathing steady.

She felt numb as she took the shirt and started toward the sink in the bathroom. Had she stared too long? Had he noticed? *Oh please, don't let him have noticed!* She turned the faucet up high and began scrubbing at the shirt with all her might.

"I don't know," he was saying, and there he was right behind her again, looking into the mirror over her head and dabbing at the wound. "What do you think? Iodine? Mercurochrome?"

She turned to look at his cut, but he was standing much too close and all she could look at was the golden skin, the stunning muscles. Could she actually feel the heat from his body? He smelled so good, like soap and fresh-cut grass. For just a moment, she was overwhelmed by the need to touch him. It swept over her in a choking wave and she felt herself yearning toward him. Every part of her wanted to feel that beautiful flesh.

It had been far too long since a man had held her in his arms.

"Oh!" she cried, turning back. "Go out," she ordered, staring down at the white shirt still in the sink and pointing toward the door.

"What's the matter?"

"You're like…naked!"

"I'm not naked. I just don't have a shirt on."

She closed her eyes and took a deep breath. "You're naked. Either you go out or I will."

He was about to say something. She could feel him revving up for it. He was either going to blast her for being ridiculous or tease her for being a ninny. She gritted her teeth, getting ready for it.

But to her relief, he resisted the temptation and quietly left the room. She sighed, knowing she'd given the game away. But there had been nothing else she could have done, except maybe to run screaming from the room herself.

It wasn't really him, she told herself a bit hysterically. It was just…well, she was a woman, after all. And he was the most gorgeous man she'd been this close to in a long, long time. Still, she wished she hadn't revealed herself that way.

She finished washing his shirt and when she came out into the office, she found him pulling on a T-shirt he'd found somewhere. It hugged his bulges and emphasized his assets, but it was better than his being naked.

"I hung your shirt on a hook in the bathroom to dry," she told him without meeting his gaze.

He turned to look at her, reminded immediately of what he liked about her. She was efficient and to the point. Her smile didn't drip with saccharin and she didn't bat her eyes. He'd been surprised at the way she'd reacted a few minutes before. Usually she was almost as careful and controlled as he was.

And that was why he'd thought she might be interested in a business proposition he'd put to her a few months before. She'd responded as though he'd asked her to sign over her soul to him and he thought she'd overreacted. Still, he hadn't been able to get the possibility out of his mind ever since.

"Am I allowed this close to you?" he teased.

"As long as you're dressed," she said calmly, flashing a sharp look his way. "Naked men make me nervous."

"Me, too," he said. "Naked women, on the other hand…"

"Should obviously be kept out of your reach."

He laughed. "Don't get the wrong idea. I'm just a tame family man." Reality flashed into his mind and his smile faded. He had no family anymore.

"Or at least I used to be," he murmured softly, staring into space.

Funny. It had been almost two years since Jan had died. There were now times when he could go a few days without the wave of nausea, the sharp pain in his heart and the cramping of his stomach muscles at the thought of her and what he'd lost. And then it would come again, slapping him in the face when he least expected it. Like now.

She was the only woman he'd ever loved or ever could love. And because of that, he almost welcomed the pain. Anything that would bring her closer for a moment. He would never get over it. He didn't want to get over it. Jan was still his wife, now and forever.

On the other hand, he ached for a child. His little Lisa had been as beloved as a baby could be and he missed her almost as much as he missed Jan. But over the last year or so, the need for another child had been growing in him. He wanted a son. A baby to fill up the hole in his heart. A child to give him a future.

"Are you thinking this way because of Granddad?" his sister, Gena, had asked him just the other day when he'd hinted at his longing. "I know he's on all the time about wanting you to marry again so you can have a son to carry on the name."

"'Grant Carver, the name of Texas heroes'," he quoted his grandfather in a voice very like his, and they both laughed. "No, this has nothing to do with getting married."

"Children usually come with mothers attached," she'd warned him.

She meant a wife, of course. She thought he ought to look for someone to marry.

"I'll find a way around that," he'd told his sister artlessly.

"You can't have a baby without getting married," she'd insisted.

"Oh, yeah? Watch me."

But he wasn't as confident as he pretended. He'd looked into the various options open to him and had found it wasn't as easy as you might think. You couldn't just order up a new kid the way he'd bought his new Lamborghini. Not if you wanted the child to actually carry your genes.

And that was what he wanted—deeply, passionately, with all his heart. He just wasn't sure how he was going to be able to make it happen.

"Do you have any family around you?" he asked Callie curiously. He knew she was a widow, but he didn't know much else about her circumstances. "Any parents or aunts and uncles?"

She had the look of someone who was thinking of edging toward the door.

"Family?" she repeated. "Uh…no, not really. I'm pretty much alone."

Leaning against his desk, he dabbed at the blood on his lip again. "Everybody needs some sort of family," he advised her. "I just spent the last few days at a friend's family reunion in San Antonio. Watching all those people enjoy each other and care about each other and depend on each other really brought it home to me. We all need other people in our lives."

And I need a son.

He didn't say it aloud, but somehow he almost felt she heard his thoughts. Watching her eyes change, he knew she was thinking of the same thing he was—of that rainy fall day about six months before when he'd nipped into his cousin's medical clinic and found Callie Stevens sitting in the waiting room.

Babies—that was his cousin's business. Ted ran an infertility clinic that specialized in in vitro fertilization. Tortured by his longing for a child to love, Grant had stopped in to see if he could get some information from his cousin about surrogate mothering—without actually planning to come clean on why he was asking about it.

And there was Callie, flipping nervously through a food magazine. He'd nodded in recognition. She'd turned beet-red and nodded back, then pretended fascination in tofu recipes. And he'd left without the information he'd come for, but with a new curiosity in just what a woman like Callie had been doing in his cousin's waiting room.

As a widow, could it be that she, like him, longed for a baby but didn't want the complications of another relationship? The thought was tantalizing and he'd spun a whole scenario around it, getting more and more enthusiastic. His cousin's office wasn't the first place he'd gone to find out about surrogates. He'd gone as far as to interview candidates at two other clinics. And he hadn't been impressed. But if he could interest a woman like Callie Stevens...

He knew instinctively she would never have a baby for mere money. So what could he do to provide an incentive? He'd mulled it over for days and thought he'd come up with a plan that would be mutually advantageous. She obviously wanted a baby. He could provide the support for her if she had a child for him—and then stayed on to basically be the child's nanny. That way they both could get what they wanted.

It sounded good to him.

The next day he called her into his office and ran it past her. She'd acted like he was setting up a baby smuggling ring and wanted her to provide the baby. She couldn't get out of his office fast enough. He was actually afraid she might quit her job or file some kind of harassment suit.

She hadn't done that, but she had acted very wary around him for a while. He hadn't brought it up again. But the possibilities were provocative, and he'd done his share of wondering—what if?

CHAPTER TWO

"You're bleeding again," Callie said, jerking Grant's attention back to the present situation. "We really need to do something about it. You need a doctor."

"Oh, no," he said, dabbing at the wound. "I can do this myself."

"No, you can't." She shook her head in exasperation. "I know you're a control freak, but you can't control everything yourself. There's a time to admit when you need help."

His blue eyes rose and held her gaze. There was nothing warm there, no teasing, no humor.

"What makes you think you know me, Ms. Callie Stevens?"

"I don't really know you, Mr. Grant Carver, but I know your type." She was on a roll. Things seemed to work much better when she took the initiative. He was scary in his way, but he could be tamed. At least, she hoped so.

"My type? Please, enlighten me. What is my type?"

She tried to glare at him but it didn't come off. He looked strangely vulnerable in the T-shirt with his mouth still bleeding. Like a fighter after a fight. All his hard edges were blurring a bit.

"Go on," he pressed. "I want to know what you think 'my type' is."

"Okay." She raised her chin. "Type A for arrogant. Type C for controlling. Type T for tyrant. Should I go on?"

"I get the picture. You don't like me very much, do you?"

She blinked at him and words stuck in her throat. Like him? What did that have to do with it? She didn't really know him, just as he'd said. What right did she have to be name-calling? Suddenly she regretted that she'd let herself tumble down this blind alley.

His handkerchief was soaked with blood and he was fishing in his desk for another one. The cut seemed to be getting worse the more he fooled with it.

She frowned. "I think you should sit down while we figure out what to do about your face," she said.

He looked up at her with a spark of humor in his eyes. "You don't like my face, either?" he said, managing to make it sound pathetic in a way guaranteed to touch her heartstrings.

She bit her lip to keep from smiling at him.

"Sit down," she said.

"I don't need to sit down, I…"

Reaching out, she flattened her hand against his chest and gave him a shove into the large leather desk chair behind him. He let her do it and didn't resist, sinking down into the leather and watching her curiously, as though he was interested in what she thought she was going to do with him next.

"Now pick up the phone and call a doctor," she ordered.

He gave her a skeptical look. "Be serious."

"I'm serious as a heart attack. You need help. I'm not leaving you here to bleed to death in the night. Pick up that phone."

"At the rate my blood is flowing, it'll take a week to bleed to death," he scoffed. But he did glance at the soaked handkerchief. Still, he hesitated. "Listen, my sister's a general practitioner. She can take care of it— if I decide that's necessary."

She motioned toward the telephone. "Call her."

"What are you talking about? It's after ten o'clock. I can't call her."

"Call her. She won't mind."

His dark eyebrows rose. "Do you know her?"

She gave him a tight smile. "I know sisters."

He stared at her for a long moment, and then something changed in his face.

"All right."

He picked up his cell and punched in a code, then put it to his ear. "Hi, Gena. It's Grant. Sorry to call so late, hon. No, nothing's wrong. I just wanted to say 'hi' and…"

It must have been because he didn't see the move coming that she was able to get the phone away from him so easily. It obviously hadn't occurred to him that

anyone would do such a thing. But she could tell his
conversation with his sister was going nowhere, so she
turned, zeroed in on her target and snatched the receiver
right out of his unsuspecting hand, then quickly moved
out of his reach while she pressed it to her ear.

"Hi, Gena. This is Callie Stevens."

"What the…?" he growled.

She waved away his rude expletive.

"You don't know me. I work…er, I used to work for
your brother. I just wanted to let you know that he's just
had an accident…."

Grant swore again, but she ignored it.

"No, no, he's fine. But he is…damaged, so to speak."
She made a face at him. "He's got a cut lip and it looks
like it needs stitches to me. It keeps bleeding, and… Oh,
great. Yes, we're at the office. Thanks."

She handed him back his telephone and gave him a
superior smile. "She's coming right over."

"What?"

"She said she's only minutes away."

"Wait one dang-burned second here," he said, his
blue eyes frosty. "I'm getting confused. Who got fired
today, you or me?"

The superior smile was working, so she kept it up.
"You'll be taken care of. So I figure we're even now.
And I'm leaving."

His expression hardened. "Not yet. The key, please."
He held out his hand.

She bit her lip and tried to look innocent. "What key?"

"The one you must have used to get into the building tonight."

Oh, that key.

It was one she'd had for opening the office early a few months before and she'd found it with her things when she'd gone through the boxes of stuff from her desk. Reaching into her pocket, she pulled it out and handed it to him.

"Wait a minute," he said. "I need to talk to you."

She turned toward the door. "Write me a letter."

He rose and followed her. "I'm quite serious. I've got something I need to discuss with you. I've got some ideas on ways we could use you here at ACW. How would you like your job back?"

There was a certain sense of satisfaction in hearing his words. This was almost an apology, wasn't it? At any rate, it was an admission that she shouldn't have been fired.

Yeah. That and a quarter will get you a ride on a pony. Big deal.

She turned back and studied his eyes. "You could do that?"

"Of course. I wouldn't have let my uncle fire you in the first place if I'd known his plans. I've been out of the office all week, as you know, and I only found out that he'd scuttled the entire research department when I got back this afternoon."

She hesitated, considering. "What makes you think I would want to come back to a place that's treated me so shabbily?"

He looked pained. "Please, no more self-righteous speeches. I thought you desperately needed this job. What happened to all your tales of woe?"

She started to speak, then thought better of it and shook her head. But she turned back, because she'd forgotten her orchid again. It would be completely ridiculous to leave it behind after all the trouble she'd taken to get it.

"You weren't really lobbying to get your job back, were you?" he said, eyes narrowing. "You were just trying to make me feel bad. Is that it?"

She looked up at him and didn't answer. What could she say? He was only partly right.

For some reason, this seemed to anger him. His hand gripped her arm, fingers curling around it.

"Just between you and me, Ms. Stevens," he said coolly, staring down into her eyes in a way that made her heart pound, "I *don't* feel bad. I never do."

Her breath caught in her throat. She prepared to yank her arm away from his grip, but he released her before she had the chance.

"Just be here first thing in the morning," he said. He glanced at the open calendar on his desk. "Oh, wait. Damn. I've got a couple of important meetings in the morning. It'll have to be after lunch." He looked up at her. "How about two o'clock? Right here in my office."

She couldn't muster any more of the superior smile shtick. Her lips were beginning to ache. So she made do with a superior shrug. "I'll think about it."

He saw right through her facade. "I'm sure you will,"

he said, his voice tinged with just a touch of sarcasm.
"And while you're at it, think about this." He gathered
her pot shards and the still-perky orchid plant and
stuffed them into a drawer in his desk. "You don't get
your orchid unless you show up."

She sprang toward him, as though to rescue her plant,
but he was ready for her this time and she stopped
herself at the last second to avoid another close contact
with his large, hard body.

"You can't do that," she cried in outrage. "That's
my property!"

It was his turn to try the superior smile.

"And you are here after breaking into *my* property.
So I guess we're even again."

She felt like pouting. Jaw rigid, she held out her
hand. "May I have my orchid, please?" she said.

"You know, I don't think I'm going to let you take it."

She glared at him. "That's despicable."

A half smile was curving his full lips. "I think I'm
going to hang on to it to make sure you come back
tomorrow."

"That's…that's like blackmail."

He considered her charge. "No, more like bribery."

"Whatever. It's illegal."

He smiled. "So sue me."

"I just might do that," she said, though they both
knew there wasn't a chance in the world of that happening. "And you know what? If I'd had the chance, I'm
sure I *would* have fired you."

And with that nonsensical statement of defiance, she turned and stormed off, taking the stairs again because she needed to work out her anger on something physical in order to keep from killing the man.

It was long past midnight. Grant still sat behind his desk, staring moodily at the dark window. His sister, Gena, had come and gone, working her medical magic, and now half of his face felt numb. But that wasn't what had him brooding. His encounter with Callie was nagging at him like a burr under a saddle. He'd mulled it over and he'd come to a decision.

Callie Stevens was the perfect woman to have his baby.

He remembered when he'd brought it up to her before. Her reaction had been extreme in his opinion. She was so calm and logical about most things. Why wasn't she logical about this? The entire plan the way he'd presented it to her would be to her benefit—that was just so obvious. And yet he knew if he came at her from that perspective again, she would react just as irrationally as she had before.

There was only one thing for it: he had to figure out how to appeal to her better nature and get her to see things his way. What was he going to do if she didn't show up tomorrow at two o'clock? What if she decided that she didn't really want to work for him and her orchid wasn't worth another run-in?

He couldn't wait for that. He would have to go to her before she had a chance to develop a real program of opposition. He didn't know where she lived but there must be a record of that in the files.

That was what he would do. He looked at his couch and grimaced. He would catch a few hours' sleep, take a shower in the washroom and take her orchid plant to her. That would make a good excuse. He shouldn't have kept it anyway. That was a foolish thing to do and he regretted it. He would stop off and pick up some doughnuts to take along as a peace offering. Just a friendly visit. That way he could get the lay of the land, see how things were with her where she lived. Maybe get an idea from her situation. Become friends with the woman.

He shrugged. It was worth a try.

"So, is he incredibly sexy?"

Tina Ramos was keeping a straight face, but the mischievous light in her dark eyes gave her away. She sat on the well-worn couch, her legs folded in around her, a cup of steaming coffee in her hands.

Callie stared at the friend who shared her apartment with her. They were sitting in the living room, watching Tina's thirteen-month-old daughter play with a round plastic toy on the floor in front of them. Callie had just finished telling Tina about what had happened the night before when she'd gone in search of her abandoned plant.

"Sexy? What? Who?" Despite her words, she knew she sounded artificially dismissive. She wasn't fooling anyone.

"Grant Carver, of course," Tina said with affected nonchalance. "We already know he's incredibly handsome."

Callie was astonished. "Oh, really? And just how do 'we' know that? I've never said a thing about his looks."

"And never noticed either, I suppose."

"Well…"

"Oh, come on, Callie." Tina was laughing. "You should see the way you look when you talk about him."

"That's crazy!" Blood was rushing to her cheeks. She could feel it. It had to be because this line of conversation was so darn annoying. Had to be. "I've never thought twice about the man."

Tina's eyes sparkled. "Oh, is that it? I guess I mistook the look."

"I guess you did." She threw up her hands and wailed, "Tina…!"

"Oh, I'm just teasing." Tina raised an eyebrow. "Are you going to the meeting?"

"Of course not."

"Why not?"

Callie hesitated, unwilling to admit aloud that it was exactly because he was sexy and he was handsome that she didn't relish going. There was something strangely compelling about the man and that made her uncomfortable. She'd built herself a little island and she fended men off with a virtual firehose. But he was the sort of man who might walk right through the blast, damp but undaunted. And mostly, she was afraid that she might let him.

"I have other things to do," she said, knowing it sounded lame, but that it had the advantage of actually being true. "I have to go out to Shady Meadows Rest

Home and see my mother-in-law. I'm hoping I can talk them into keeping her where she is for just one more month while I try to scrape up enough money to transfer her to full nursing care."

"Scraping together money isn't going to be easy now that you've lost both jobs," Tina said, her eyes losing their sparkle quickly.

Callie sighed. "I will go out and see him later," she said, knowing it was childish to go late, just because he wanted her to come at two. But when you came right down to it, she did need the job. She had to go.

Tina hesitated, then reached out and took her friend's hand. "Callie, I called the agency last night and told them to double my assignments. If I can make a bit more…"

Callie winced. Tina was trained as an elementary teacher, but after a cancer scare, she'd taken up cleaning houses for a living, working for an agency part-time and making just enough to get by on.

"No, Tina. You need to be home with your baby while you can be."

Tina pressed a finger to her lips. "I'm taking her with me," she whispered.

Callie groaned. "You're not allowed to do that and you know it."

Tina shrugged. "No one's turned me in yet. Everyone loves having Molly around."

Callie glanced down at the beautiful child. Of course everyone loved Molly. What was there not to love? With her head of shining chocolate-colored curls and her huge dark eyes, so alive and so interested in everything, she was as fresh and pure as a snowflake.

The little darling had certainly turned Callie's life around. Tina and Molly had come to live with her just before Christmas and nothing had been the same since. There was joy in her life now. Joy, and a beautiful baby.

It wasn't her baby, and it was only temporary—like everything else in her life. But that didn't really matter right now. A life that had been cold and lonely for years had become warm again. She'd been searching for something to live for. She'd even looked into having a baby on her own. The hunger for a child was deep and raw inside her. But no matter which way she turned, she couldn't seem to manage to find a way to do it that made sense. Now, with her own little rag-tag family, she had something. At least for the moment.

Rising, she started toward the kitchen but the sound of the doorbell startled them all.

"I'll get it," Tina said, heading for the door.

Callie frowned, wondering who it could be and smoothing back her hair. She'd thrown on a big purple sweatshirt and an old pair of baggy jeans when she'd rolled out of bed. She thought she remembered brushing her thick hair, but it felt a little wild at the moment. She wasn't really ready for company, especially not…

Grant Carver.

"I hope I'm not intruding," he was saying as Tina let him in.

And then there he was, handsome and sexy, just as

Tina had surmised—if a bit wounded. His lip was swollen and that side of his face was slightly discolored. Callie winced, looking at him. And then she wondered once again why the injury made him look so much more appealing. Did she feel a natural attraction to damaged men?

Carrying a large Stetson, he was dressed for the office, very sharp and very elegant—while she knew she must look like a refugee from the hill country.

Was he intruding? Oh, yes, very definitely.

"Oh, no, not at all," Tina said quickly when Callie didn't answer him right away. She threw him a bright smile that spoke volumes as to her opinion of the way he presented himself. "I'm Tina, the roommate. We've been up for hours. Just talking, you know. About…" She stopped and bit her lip, looking guilty as sin.

"About?" he asked, waiting.

"About things," Tina said with a sigh and a quick look of apology toward Callie. They all knew that he knew he'd been the object of their conversation.

"'Shoes and ships and sealing wax'?" he quoted helpfully.

"Oh, yes. Those things, too." She smiled at him. "Cabbages and kings. All that stuff."

"Wonderful." He held out one of two bags he carried with him. "I brought doughnuts, just in case."

"Lovely," Tina cried, taking it from him. "How do you take your coffee?"

"Black, thanks."

"I'll be just a moment."

"Take your time," he said, turning slowly to look at the room and wondering what the hell he was doing here.

Well…bringing Callie back her orchid plant. That was the official objective. And to take the first steps toward becoming friends. But now that he was here, he realized he might be walking into a trap of his own making.

And then he looked at Callie and he was sure of it.

Crazy. That was the only word for it. He was crazy. Just being here went against every rule and every plan he'd made for himself.

He hadn't been able to get her out of his mind. He told himself it was because she represented such possibilities. Looking at her, he knew it was more than that. And now he knew something else.

The efficient, no-nonsense Callie he was used to at work fascinated and intrigued him. But there was another Callie. This one had sleepy eyes and a thoroughly kissable mouth and hair that glowed like a wild, golden cloud around her pretty face. No makeup. Bare feet. Lovely breasts that were emphasized by the way the cloth of her sweatshirt draped across them.

And suddenly he felt something he hadn't felt for a long, long time. Deep, hungry, carnal desire.

He looked away quickly. Wow. This was no good. He didn't want to feel sexually attracted, not like this. He needed distance so as to keep control.

"Hey," he said, nodding to her and looking stormy on purpose. "I had a hell of a time finding you."

"Really?" She shrugged nonchalantly. "And here I didn't even know I was lost."

"Oh, you were lost all right. At least to me. The employee card I used had your old address."

She looked incredulous. "So you went to Buckaroo Court, looking for me?"

"Yeah." He made a face. "Not exactly the garden spot of Dallas, is it?"

She sighed. "Not exactly. Which is why I moved over here as soon as I could."

He nodded, and she frowned.

"And someone told you my new address?"

"Yes." One dark eyebrow rose. "A semidelightful gentleman named Butch. He was throwing soapy water on his motorcycle in the driveway but kindly took a break to give me your whereabouts."

"The so-called manager." She shuddered. "More like the game warden." Giving him a wise look, she added, "How much did he stick you for?"

"A cool twenty got me the information. I thought it was a bargain."

She winced, eyes sparkling. "Yikes. I guess I'm going cheap these days."

He shrugged. "I got a discount after I roughed him up a little."

She gasped, then didn't know whether to take him seriously or not. "You didn't!"

He gave her a half smile, not ready to satisfy her curiosity. "Enough about Butch. He's not very interesting anyway. I brought you your orchid." He held up a brown paper bag and peeled back enough to show her a flower peeking from inside.

"So I see," she said, looking at it warily, then shifting to look up into his eyes. "What do you want for it?"

He gave her a pained look. "See, that's exactly why I brought it to you. I decided you were right. It wasn't fair to hold your orchid as bait to draw you back. I ought to have enough faith in you to assume you'll do the right thing without having to be coerced."

"Thank you." She snatched up her plant, hugged it to her chest, then looked at him gingerly. "But you see, that's where you make your big mistake. Now that I've got my plant…"

"You'll be so grateful, you'll probably come early and camp on my doorstep," he said, but his expression was cynical.

And she suppressed a smile. "Dream on."

She peeked inside the bag. The orchid looked as though it enjoyed car trips. That was a relief. Her orchid was no longer held hostage.

Setting it down on the tiled window ledge alongside two others, she turned back to Grant. His lower lip looked even more swollen from this side and she could see evidence of stitches, though they were just about invisible. At least he'd let his sister take care of his injury.

"What happened to your important meetings?" she asked.

"I'll make them. I only stopped by for a moment."

Tina brought out coffee and doughnuts on a plate, prattling with small talk all the while. Callie and Grant sat cautiously on the couch, eyeing each other like two gunslingers meeting at the corral, each waiting for the other to move toward the doughnuts first.

Watching them, Tina grinned, then scooped up her baby, who was sucking on a red lollipop, and turned back to say goodbye.

"We're going to the park," she explained.

"Oh, don't go!" Callie cried fervently.

But Tina merely gave her a wink. "We'll be back soon."

Callie hardly noticed the wink, because she was caught up in watching Grant's reaction to Molly. He took one look at her and recoiled as though something had stung him. It was quickly apparent that he wanted to be as far away from the baby as he could get.

Tina didn't seem to notice, and neither did Molly. The little girl gazed at him intently, then her chubby arms shot out as though asking him to take her from her mom.

"Da Da!" she cried, her eyes lighting up.

"No, honey," Tina said, laughing. "That's not your da da."

Turning, she looked back over her shoulder at Callie.

"More's the pity," she muttered with a significant look. And then the two of them were out the door.

Grant reached out and took a piece of doughnut in his hand, then popped it into his mouth.

"So you live here with Tina," he noted, reaching for his coffee next.

"And Molly," Callie said. "Our little angel."

He winced and avoided her gaze. At a glance, the little girl had looked just like Lisa. And thinking about Lisa was the one thing that rendered him helpless. He didn't want to hear about Molly, or anything else that reminded him of his own baby.

"What does Tina do?"

She gave him a suspicious sideways look. "Why do you want to know?"

"I'm interested in you and your life."

She turned to frown at him. "Why?"

He shrugged in exasperation. "Weren't you the one telling me that you and your fellow workers were real human beings with real lives and not chess pieces? I'm trying to learn to be a better boss. I'm empathizing."

For a moment, he thought she was going to laugh in his face.

"Right," she said skeptically. "Okay, Mr. Sensitive, empathize this. Tina is a wonderful person. My best friend. She's had some bad luck and hard knocks, and right now she's in and out of remission of her cancer and trying to raise her baby on her own."

"That's insane," he interjected coolly. "A woman with that sort of health danger has no business having a child."

Her eyes widened and she looked at him as though he were a freak. "Sometimes these things are beyond our control."

"Nothing's ever beyond control."

"Oh brother." She rose from the couch and picked up her coffee cup. "You're so wrong. I've been on a runaway roller coaster for years and I still haven't found the brakes on the darn thing."

"Maybe I can help you with that," he said softly.

She stared at him and he stared right back. She tried so hard to keep a mask of quiet competence in place, but he was beginning to see through it. She wasn't as good at hiding as she thought.

She went into the kitchen to refill her cup and he followed her.

She turned, startled. "Did you want more coffee?" she asked.

"No, thanks," he said. "I've got to get going."

She looked up at him and his gaze went to her mouth, then veered quickly away.

"I'll be expecting you at two," he said, picking up his hat.

"Why?" she asked simply.

He turned back and looked at her. "Because I want to talk over some possibilities with you. I told you I wanted to find a way to get you back at work at ACW."

She frowned, obviously suspicious. "Why do you care whether it's me or someone else?"

He stopped dead, staring at her. "Callie, why don't you trust me?"

"I trust you."

"No, you don't. You're suspicious of everything I say and do."

"That's not really true."

"What have I done to make you so wary? Or has someone else hurt you?"

Bingo. He saw it in her eyes. But she wasn't going to admit it.

"This is ridiculous," she said, turning away. "I like you better as a boss than a therapist."

"Then we agree," he said, turning to follow her.

She passed so close he thought he caught the scent of her hair. She was very real, very flesh and blood. She put up a lot of barricades and hid behind defenses, but there was nothing coy or artificial about her.

He liked her. He liked the way she looked and the way she walked and the way she held her head when she talked to him so seriously. He actually liked that she was wary of him. He wouldn't have respected her if she'd jumped at the things he said too eagerly. She was pretty and smart and classy.

Yes. He had to have her as the mother of his child. She was perfect. She was the one.

"Will you come?" he asked, resisting the impulse to grab her and sling her over his shoulder.

She looked at him. "I'll think about it."

"Two o'clock sharp."

"I know. I got that."

He went to the door. "If you don't show up..."

"You'll come back and torture my orchid?" she suggested lightly.

"No." He favored her with a slow grin. "But I will be back."

He left whistling. She would come. For curiosity's sake if nothing else.

CHAPTER THREE

IT FELT odd walking down the corridors where Callie had been an employee only one day before. People glanced up and did a double-take when they saw her. She smiled and held her head high. A few smiled back but she hadn't made many friends outside of her own department—and they were all gone.

Lynnette, Grant Carver's administrative assistant, didn't smile. She rose from her desk and ushered Callie into Grant's office immediately, but she didn't look happy to do it.

The woman thinks I'm some sort of gold digger, Callie guessed perceptively. Oh well. She was protective of her boss and Callie supposed that was a good thing.

Grant rose in a courtly manner and shook hands with her, establishing the businesslike mood right away. He wore beautiful wool slacks and a crisp white shirt with a sky-blue tie—the picture of the ideal entrepreneur.

"Please have a seat, Ms. Stevens," he said, gesturing

toward the chair he'd pulled up before the desk. "I'm glad you decided to come."

"Thank you." She sat down feeling nervous and wondering why she'd let herself wear such a short skirt. No wonder Lynnette was leery.

"Well, let's get right to it," he said, barely glancing at her shapely legs before shuffling papers on his desk. "Looking over your record, I see you've had a few prelaw courses in college. Were you planning to go to law school?"

She hesitated. Her past was tangled with twists and turns she didn't want to get into. "At one point, I had hopes along those lines," she admitted.

He nodded, his gaze cool and reserved. Looking at him, she could hardly believe this was the same man she'd fallen on the night before, the same man who'd thrown her for a loop by taking his shirt off, the same man who'd appeared on her doorstep with doughnuts.

"ACW Properties has a couple of openings, but the one I would think best for you would be a position in the paralegal section of our law department," he was saying. "Perhaps you'd be interested."

"I don't have any paralegal training," she said quickly. "Don't they usually want a certificate for that?"

He nodded, his wide mouth twitching at the corners. "They might. But I think I can get a waiver on that. Even personnel tends to do what I tell them to."

"Oh. Of course." He was the boss, after all. She just wasn't used to getting favored treatment from anyone.

"You would start out as an assistant to our paralegal staff," he said. "We would expect you to develop quickly into a fully qualified paralegal. Here's the projected salary."

He wrote the number on a piece of paper and passed it to her. Her eyes widened as she noted the sum.

"It's a nice raise," he said.

She looked across the desk, trying to read something in his eyes. It *was* a nice raise. Too nice. What did he really want?

"This is more than I expected," she said mistrustfully. "What are you going to want me to do for it?"

His eyes glittered and she realized what she'd at first taken for irritation was actually humor.

"So young and yet so cynical," he said. "I expect you to do a good job for ACW. A very good job."

She frowned, searching his eyes. She was usually pretty good at reading people, but for some reason she couldn't get a handle on his moods and motives today.

"I don't get it," she challenged. "This is too much money for a job that's actually an assistant to an assistant."

He shrugged. "Why don't you turn it down, then?" he said softly, watching her like a cat watching a mouse.

"Heck no," she said, tossing her hair back and looking him straight in the eye. "I need the money badly. I just want to make sure I know what the money is actually buying before I agree to take it."

"I expect top-notch work and I'm willing to pay for quality."

Funny, but she was still uneasy, feeling there was something behind what he was saying, something he was holding back. His comment about being willing to pay for quality seemed to have an added significance she just wasn't getting.

"I won't disappoint you," she said.

He nodded slowly, but his eyes seemed to be seeing right through her. She waited a moment, then added a question.

"Well then, shall I start tomorrow?"

"Tomorrow?"

She frowned. What was the matter with him? He was gazing at her blankly as though his mind was a million miles away.

"Hello," she said, waving a hand before his eyes.

"Oh, sure," he said quickly, realizing he'd been drifting away from the conversation. "Tomorrow would be fine."

He ran a hand through his thick hair, staring at her. His mind hadn't been a million miles away at all. It had been right here, trying to figure out how he was going to bring up the baby thing as he'd planned to. Why couldn't he seem to get together the right words to ask her? It had to be done. It needed to be done. And here he was, at a loss as to how he was going to do it.

This wasn't like him. He never lacked ideas, never shrank from difficult subjects. He went after what he wanted with a singular confidence some even labeled as arrogance. It hadn't even occurred to him that he would have trouble putting what he wanted into words. But here he was, struggling—and running through different options with no clue.

What should he say? How should he approach it? With humor? Seriousness? Casual unconcern?

Uh...Ms. Stevens? One more thing. You can qualify for a big bonus if you agree to have my baby.

Oh, yeah. That would work.

Ms. Stevens, in looking over your records, I see that you would be the perfect person to have my baby. What do you say?

He winced, knowing very well what she would say to that and not wanting to hear it aloud.

Ms. Stevens, I'm sure you know that the Carver family looms large in the history of Texas. We weren't at the Alamo, but we were just about everywhere else. The tragedy is, I am the last in the Grant Carver line, and I need to have a son to carry on the name and the legacy. You seem to be uniquely qualified and have been selected for this honor... If you would like to contribute to the cause of Texas history...

Oh hell, that wouldn't work, either. Why couldn't he think of anything workable?

But maybe it was just as well. He was probably rushing things. Maybe it would be better to give it a few weeks, to let her get comfortable with him, maybe even start to trust him a little. Maybe...

"Is there something else?" She was looking at him curiously.

He sighed. "No. Not yet."

"Not yet?"

"I mean... No. Thank you for coming in. I'll make sure personnel has your paperwork ready in the morning."

"Fine. I'll see you later, then." She rose. "And thank you, Mr. Carver. I appreciate this."

Rising as well, he shook hands with her and said, "Till tomorrow, then."

She threw him a last puzzled look and turned to go. It was pure fancy, he knew, but some of the light seemed to dim as she left the room.

"Hey, Mr. Carver."

He looked up to find Darren Evans, a bright young lawyer who had recently been hired, entering his office but looking back at where Callie was disappearing into the elevator.

"Pretty lady," he noted, one eyebrow raised as he gestured toward her.

"Yes." Grant frowned as Darren dumped a stack of contracts on his desk. He seemed to be a pretty good lawyer, but his reputation as a ladies' man was beginning to loom larger than his talent.

"I heard she's a widow. Is that right?"

"That's right." Grant's frown deepened. "Why do you ask?"

"I just wanted to make sure." Darren had a young man's casual confidence in his own irresistibility. "I was thinking about asking her out."

"I'm afraid you're a little late for that," Grant said

without a second of hesitation. Every male instinct in him rose up in a makeshift defensive posture.

"Oh, yeah?"

"Yes. She's not available."

"Really? Who…?"

"Darren, that's really none of your business."

"Oh. Okay." He sighed. "That's a shame. Early bird gets the worm, huh?"

Grant scowled at him. Darren finally seemed to notice that his boss wasn't pleased with his company and bowed out quickly, but Grant's mind was churning. What Darren said had opened his eyes a bit. He was beginning to realize he couldn't fool around waiting for the right moment with Callie. If he didn't get a commitment from her soon, she might just fall prey to some playboy like Darren Evans. He had to think of a way to approach her with it. Very soon.

But he wasn't going to think of anything just sitting here. Rising, he shoved his hands deep into his pockets and began pacing the floor. Going to the window, he looked down. And there she was. Callie had stopped at the courtyard fountain and was gazing down into the water.

Now. He had to go now before he lost this chance. Turning on his heel, he raced out of the office, past a startled Lynnette, past the elevator, straight for the stairs. Taking them two at a time, he sailed down six floors like a downhill skier on powder, bursting out into the courtyard at full tilt and coming to a quick stop. She was still there. He was going to do it and he was going to do it now.

As he walked up behind her, he took in her trim form, her slender neck, the way her hair tumbled down her back. This was the woman he wanted as the mother of his child. And suddenly he knew that, once again, where Callie was concerned, all his plans were sailing out the window.

Had he really contemplated asking a woman like this to have his child without offering her marriage? Was he nuts? He couldn't insult her that way. Maybe that was what had been inhibiting him—knowing it wouldn't work no matter how gracefully he tried to put it. If he was going to do this thing, he was going to have to go all the way.

"Callie," he said, and she turned, startled, and stared up at him, her mouth slightly open.

"Callie Stevens…" He took her hand in his and gazed down earnestly into her dark eyes. "Will you marry me?"

Tina was sitting in the middle of the living room rug, rolling a ball to Molly.

"You're home already?" Callie said as Molly ran to greet her with little baby kisses. "I thought you were taking two jobs today."

Tina was smiling, but her face was strained. "I got so tired, I just couldn't go to the second one. I… I'm sorry, Callie. I know I promised you."

"Oh, Tina, please! If you feel the least bit tired, you are to come home immediately! Don't think twice. We don't want you getting really sick. Molly needs you. Don't you, pumpkin?"

Molly squealed as Callie tickled her tummy.

"But we need the money," Tina was saying.

"No problem," Callie said briskly, depositing the wriggling youngster in her mother's lap. "I've got an armload of newspapers. I'm going to scour the ads and get my résumé pulled together tonight, then head out onto the pavement first thing in the morning. I'll get something right away. You'll see." She smiled at her friend. "Don't you worry."

"Callie, I do worry. Things were already tight before you got laid off."

Molly was beginning to fuss and Tina whipped out a red lollipop to tempt her with.

Callie frowned. "Should you really be giving those to her? Won't they rot her teeth?"

"What teeth?" But Tina was joking. They both knew Molly was developing quite a set. "Don't worry. I usually only let her have one a day and I brush her teeth right after she finishes. And also, you'll note the stick is rubbery, so it's not dangerous." She sounded defensive as if she'd had to explain this to others before. Her smile was a bit watery. "They're her favorites. She just loves them. And I feel like she got the short end of the stick in so many ways…."

Her voice trailed off and Callie regretted having said anything. Tina had enough to worry about without her best friend criticizing the way she was raising her baby.

"How did the meeting go?" Tina said, changing the subject.

Callie hesitated, wondering how much she wanted to tell. "He offered me a job. As an assistant in paralegal."

"Great!"

Callie shook her head, feeling frazzled. Life was spinning out of control and she had to stop it somehow.

"It's no use. I can't take the job. The man is a raving lunatic."

She raised a hand to stop Tina's inevitable questions. She had to think this through before she could analyze it with her friend.

"Sorry, Tina. I really can't talk about it right now. Maybe later."

"Oh. Okay." Tina's puzzled look turned tragic. "Oh. The home called. They said they couldn't hold your mother-in-law's room any longer. Unless they get the extra fee by Friday, they are going to transfer her to the county facility."

Callie felt as though she'd been slugged in the stomach. She had to struggle not to show her dismay to Tina. Instead she took a deep-cleansing breath and tried to smile.

"Oh, Callie, if it weren't for you, she would have been there over a year ago. You're so good to her. But I've got to say, I don't understand why you've taken on such a big responsibility. Why do you feel she's your burden?"

Callie thought for a moment, wondering how she could explain. "She's my husband's mother. She was good to me."

"Your husband wasn't."

"No. But that's not really her fault." She shook her

head. "I'm the only family she has left, and she's the only family I've ever had."

Tina sighed, looking at her own little girl as she played on the floor.

"Not many daughters would be as generous as you, not to mention daughters-in-law." Tina shook her head. "Callie, you've got to look out for yourself sometimes."

"I look after myself just fine. Don't worry about me. I'm okay."

She went to the kitchen and began wiping down the counters, more because she needed to be doing something than because they needed it. Her mind was still reeling from Grant Carver's proposal. She felt as though she'd passed into an alternate universe. What he'd suggested was insane. Impossible. Outrageous.

"Will you marry me?" he'd said, and she almost fell into the fountain.

At first she'd thought he must be joking. Or playing some sort of wicked game. But he'd been so sincere and spoken so earnestly, she quickly realized he meant it. He wanted to marry her—and more. He wanted her to have a baby for him.

She supposed that shouldn't be so shocking. After all, he'd brought it up before. She'd been trying to forget that offer ever since. He'd thought she could have a baby for him and then be the baby's nanny. Fat chance! That had been just a little too cold-blooded for her and she'd told him so.

But now he'd upped the ante. He'd brought marriage into it.

And yet, what difference did that make? He was still basically proposing to pay her to have a baby for him. People didn't do things like that.

Well, they did, but...

He brought up that day he'd seen her in the fertility clinic, and she had to admit she'd been looking into the feasibility of having a baby with artificial insemination—that she wanted a baby just as badly as he did. That she, like him, didn't want to marry again. And that she hadn't been able to go through with it.

But that didn't mean she was ready to marry Grant Carver, no matter how hard he argued that it would be more a business proposition than a real marriage. That would be crazy.

She pulled open the refrigerator and took out an onion and some carrots. Taking them to the cutting board, she began to cut them up into small pieces, chopping hard, and at the same time, she tried to think about something else. Anything else.

But her mind had blotted everything else out. All she could think about was this insane issue.

What right did Grant have to come into her life and turn it upside down? She'd been perfectly happy... Well, maybe not perfectly happy. In fact, maybe a bit stressed. But still. He'd brought up things she didn't want to think about. Like what did she actually plan to do with her life?

Not get married. That was for sure. After all, it wasn't

as though she expected to meet her prince charming in the next few years. It had been six long years since Ralph had died and she hadn't met one man whom she would remotely consider marrying.

Okay, maybe just one. But that one was Grant Carver. So why wasn't she considering him?

Because he doesn't love you, stupid!

At least he was honest about it.

And yet, a little tiny part of her brain was whispering, "What if…?"

No!

Better a life of lonely misery than marrying a man who didn't love her.

She stopped for a moment, frowning. Was she really thinking this through? Or just spouting slogans?

Her thoughts were still swirling when a really startling epiphany popped into her head. If she did what Grant wanted, she would be making life better for four other people. And that wasn't even counting herself.

No! Impossible. There had to be another way.

She rinsed the washcloth she'd used on the counter and started toward the refrigerator, but noticed that Tina had put the mail on the kitchen table. She leafed through the envelopes. Nothing but bills. A gnawing ache had settled in the pit of her stomach.

And then she came to a note at the bottom of the stack. It was from Karen, the apartment building manager.

"Callie, I'm sorry, but I'm going to have to have this month's rent check by Friday or…"

The ache became a sharp pain and she gasped, clutching her midsection. Tears filled her eyes. She'd been close to the edge before, but this time she was hanging on by her fingernails. What was she going to do? Even if she took the job Grant had offered with its new salary, it wouldn't come close to covering all the expenses she was drowning in.

"Ca-ee."

Callie looked down. There was Molly, tugging on her skirt. She smiled at the adorable child. Grant had lost a little girl very much like this one. For just a moment, she could catch a hint of how horrible that must be for him.

Molly reached up with her chubby arms and Callie leaned down to lift her. The baby stared at the tears in Callie's eyes, then reached out and touched one on her cheek with the end of a tiny finger. Her mouth opened in surprise when her finger came back wet.

Callie laughed and let Molly wipe away the rest of her tears, one by one. Hugging her close, she dropped a kiss on the top of her curly head, marveling at how the sweetness of the child helped to wash away a lot of the fear.

She so longed for a baby of her own and holding Molly just brought that ache front and center. A baby was something real and permanent.

Everything in her life had always been so temporary. She'd never known her father. Her mother had been the sort of woman who needed a man in her life, yet couldn't keep one for more than a few months. After her mother died, she'd lived in foster homes. Nothing real, solid, enduring. Her life was always in flux with nothing to hold on to.

When she'd married Ralph, she'd thought that would be it. She would have something lasting. It hadn't taken her long to realize that hope was just as big a failure as all the others. Ralph as a suitor was very different from the man she ended up married to. Once again she was on her own.

She knew that was one reason she was so drawn to having a child. A child wasn't temporary. A child was forever. A child was tenderness and trust and a stake in destiny.

A baby filled your arms with more than soft, clean-smelling flesh. A baby filled your arms with love and happiness and hope for the future. She wanted that. She needed it.

And if she was honest, she would admit that Grant could make all that possible. And at the same time, she could make it possible for him.

She could give that to Grant.

She had the power to do it.

She could give that to herself.

Did she have the nerve to do it?

CHAPTER FOUR

NEGOTIATIONS had begun.

The setting was a trendy café with reflective surfaces and hard edges. The mood was wary and exploratory. The outcome was uncertain.

"So how would this work exactly?" Callie asked, trying very hard to be cool, calm and collected while her stomach was manufacturing butterflies in herds. "I think we should be very clear on all the details from the start, so we both know where we stand."

Grant nodded. "To start with, what we're talking about here is a business deal, not a love match," he said, gazing at her levelly across a tile-covered table.

He'd said that before. She had no doubt he was going to say it again. Many times.

"Yes. I understand that."

At least, she thought she did. When you came right down to it, she wasn't sure she knew what a "love match" was. She wasn't sure she even believed in them. When she'd married Ralph, she'd done it out of gratitude, not passion. She'd known right from the beginning that love had very little to do with it.

She didn't even think there'd been much love on Ralph's part. There had been an obsession—but it was an obsession with control. They'd gone very quickly from being good friends to wary adversaries and she wasn't sure how or why it had happened that way. She only knew she didn't want that to happen here—if she decided to do this crazy thing.

"In fact," Grant was saying, his hands curled around a large mug of coffee, "when I first started thinking about it, as you know, marriage wasn't really a part of the plan."

"Well, it is now," she said quickly. "In fact, it's a deal breaker."

He nodded. "I know. Don't worry." He smiled at her in a reassuring way. "I feel the same way, now that I've thought it through."

"Good."

She was trying hard to seem composed, but he could sense her unease and he hesitated, wanting to get this right. He'd deliberately chosen a rather noisy, modish restaurant for this meeting. He hadn't wanted white linen tablecloths and roses, with violins in the background. Techno music and hard surfaces made a better match for their purposes. It would be best to hammer out the future guidelines for their relationship in a cool, neutral atmosphere. No emotions allowed.

Yesterday had been a day from hell. He'd been so clumsy, practically assaulting her with his appeal that she marry him. He'd tried to explain, tried to tell her about his family heritage, and his own overwhelming need for a child. She thought at first that he was joking. Then she thought he was crazy. She'd placed a few well-aimed barbs in his hide and taken off, flinging a demand that he not ever, ever contact her again behind her as she left.

And who could blame her? He'd done a lousy job of making his case. So he'd spent the night pacing the floor of his penthouse apartment, trying to think of a better way to approach her. He was usually good at this sort of thing. There were some who said he could charm the socks off a cat, but his natural abilities seemed to fade away when his emotions were involved so strongly.

And that was why emotions had to be controlled, tamped down—blotted out if possible.

When she didn't show up for work in the morning, he knew he'd really made a mess of it. By noon, he'd been about to go out to her apartment and break down her door if he had to. And then Lynnette had looked into his office with news.

"There's someone here to see you," she'd said, seeming disapproving.

When Callie appeared in his doorway, his heart had been thumping so loud, he was afraid they could hear it in the lunchroom.

"I've calmed down," she said, looking at him warily. "And I'd like to talk things over."

So here they were in The ZigZag Café, surrounded by young twenty-somethings, meeting and greeting and listening to electronic music that made his teeth hurt. But they were keeping emotions out of it. Sort of.

"I think we ought to pin down just what exactly you would expect out of this," she said, putting down her café latte and looking like a lawyer ready to take a statement from the witness.

"Sure. I expect—" He stopped himself, then purposely relaxed. "No, let's put it this way. I hope for a child. With his mother attached. I hope for a warm family group. I'd like to end up with some basic emotional support, and I expect to give the same to you."

She nodded, biting her lip. "Like good friends?" she asked, looking skeptical.

"Like good friends," he agreed.

She frowned thoughtfully. That worried her. It sounded too familiar. But she didn't see an alternative.

"If I agree to do this, what happens if…" She swallowed hard and avoided his bright gaze. "What happens if it doesn't pan out?"

He had to work hard to keep from grinning at her. He could tell she was getting closer and closer to saying "yes." He drummed his fingers on the tile table to keep from showing what he was thinking, how excitement was growing in him, deep down.

"We'll negotiate an agreement to include things like that."

She managed to smile and tried to make a joke. "If

that happens, I suppose, like Henry the Eighth, you'll move on and find your Anne Boleyn somewhere."

He smiled back. "So you're channeling Catherine of Aragon now?"

She shrugged. "Better a divorce than losing my head."

He winced. "I'm having my lawyer draw up a contract," he said. "It will cover all contingencies."

"Fine. If we end up doing this, I'll have my lawyer look it over." As if she had one. Well, she would have one before things were finalized. "I'll get back to you on what changes we'll want."

He shook his head, studying her through narrowed eyes. "Why do you assume there will need to be changes?"

Her smile was brittle. "Because I'm sure this would be made from your point of view. That's only natural. But I'm bound to have my own concerns. Equal time."

He nodded slowly, reminding himself that he was going to have to take her thoughts into account. This wasn't like hiring an employee, really. It was going to be more like a partnership. That gave him a momentary qualm. He did like to be in control. But then he relaxed and congratulated himself on being so perceptive—and magnanimous.

A partnership. Of course.

Callie seemed to be reading his mind.

"You do understand that I couldn't have a baby and then just hand him over to you," she said, looking him straight in the eye. "I won't be a surrogate mother. I'd be in this for parenthood as much as you are."

"Absolutely." He frowned, trying to make out what was hidden in her eyes. "So tell me, Callie. I want to know why you're considering this. What is it that *you* expect?"

She took a deep breath. "A good father for my child. A protected situation to raise my child in."

"Exactly what I plan to provide." He was having a hard time containing himself. "Callie, we can do this thing. We can have a child together. Are you starting to feel how possible this is?"

"Maybe." She hesitated and steeled herself. Now came the hard part. "But I've got to admit, there's more. I've got to be totally honest with you. I really, really want a baby. It's a desire that almost consumes me at times. But there's another factor going into this." Taking a deep breath, she went on. "I'm in major financial difficulties right now."

There. The words were out. And she felt horrible about it. She glanced quickly at his eyes. Was he radiating contempt? Was he sneering? To her surprise, it didn't seem to be that way.

"No problem," he was saying, waving it away as though money was no object. "Just let me know what you need."

"No!" She said that a bit too loud and looked around quickly. Luckily the music had hidden her cry, but she leaned in closer. "No, really. It's not like that. What I would want to do is to keep working as long as I possibly can."

"Why would you do that?" he broke in. "You don't need to."

"Yes, I do. I can't just…"

"Callie, we'll play it by ear. Whatever feels most comfortable for you, that's what we'll do."

She closed her eyes for a moment. He was being almost too nice about this. She didn't deserve it. But then, he did want something from her.

Looking at him earnestly, she quickly tried to explain her dilemma, how she desperately needed to pay for her mother-in-law's nursing care, how she wanted to be in the position to get the best medical help possible for Tina—how she was so far in debt both goals were completely out of reach at the moment.

"So you see, all my motives are not so pure," she told him, chin high but bright spots in her cheeks. "If I do this with you, I have to know if you will be willing to help me financially. Purely as a loan," she added quickly. "Believe me, I'll pay back every penny. But if this is going to be a problem, even just a nagging thing with the potential to build…"

Watching her, he could see how hard this was for her to ask. Didn't she understand how laughably easy it would be for him to do this for her? No. In a flash of perception, he knew she *did* understand that. Still, she felt this would look like she was offering herself up for sale and she hated that.

Hey. No problem. He could take care of something so simple, so why not do it? There would be plenty of difficult things down the road. Get rid of the small stuff.

"Callie…" Reaching out across the table, he took her

hand in his and held it. "It's done. I'll have my accountant call you and arrange for what you need."

She flushed and tried to pull away, but he wouldn't let her.

"Listen to me. It's done. I won't even be personally involved." His gaze darkened. "And it's not contingent on our plans. You can walk away and think it over and decide against marrying me, and it's still done. Consider the matter closed." He smiled at her doubtful look. "Now let's get back to baby talk. What'll we name him?"

Her eyes stung and there was a sudden large lump in her throat. To think he could so casually wave a magic wand and take a weight off her shoulders that had been threatening to crush her. She wanted to thank him, but she couldn't speak. And now it was she who was holding tightly to his hand.

"Why, Grant Carver, you handsome man, you!"

They both jumped and Grant jerked away from Callie's hand as though it had suddenly turned white-hot. He looked up at the tall, beautiful woman who'd stopped by their table, then rose to his feet to greet her.

"Amy. How nice to see you."

"Oh, Grant!"

The woman came in for a hug and clung to him so long, he had to peel her off his chest.

"This is Callie Stevens," he said, looking a little grumpy and stepping back so she couldn't do that again. "Callie, this is Amy Barnes, an old friend."

Amy nodded to Callie but it was obvious she only

had eyes for Grant. As slender and sleek as a high fashion model, she was wearing a tight designer suit that had probably cost about as much as Callie's car.

"I'm here with the girls," she said, gesturing toward where three other women who could have been her clones waited, giggling and looking coy. "We're having lunch. Isn't this the most adorable place? I love the music. It just makes me want to dance." She did a little two-step to demonstrate, looking as provocative as possible. "Listen, honey, why don't you come over and say hi to the girls? They'd love it if you did."

Grant looked as though he'd been asked to eat a bug. "Uh…well, you see, Ms. Stevens and I are in a kind of a meeting about something important right now. And I'm afraid—"

"Oh." She flashed a false smile Callie's way. "Well, okay then. But you call me, ya hear? We need to get together and talk over old times. You know…" She moved closer and spoke in a hushed voice. "It's Jan's birthday next week. I think we really should—"

"I'll give you a call," he said hastily. "Give my best to the girls."

He dropped back down into his seat as she sashayed her way across the room.

"My wife's best friend," he said by way of explanation.

She nodded, glancing surreptitiously toward the women and wondering if his wife had been one of that type as well. If so, was he going to be satisfied with a complete change of pace? He was in for a major culture shock.

But she pushed that thought away, because adding it to her other doubts would put her brain on overload. She just didn't have room for more. She had a big decision to make. Whatever she decided, it was going to change her life for good.

She took a good long, penetrating look at the man sitting opposite her. Could she marry him? Could she live with him? How well did she really know him?

Well enough, she decided. Yes, she knew a lot about him when you came right down to it. And the fact that he was impossibly attractive didn't hurt. If he'd been a small, cramped, ugly man who had an annoying voice, would she have been able to marry him?

Luckily she didn't have to answer that, because no one was going to ask her.

"Okay," he was saying, glancing at his watch. "I've got to get back to the office. You go home and think it over."

"How much time do I have?"

He thought for a moment, looking at her warmly. "How about twenty-four hours?" he said. "I'll pick you up for dinner tomorrow at five. We'll talk it out then. Okay?"

She nodded slowly, then frowned. "I don't suppose you'd be up for making a list of your bad points, just so I'd have something to mull over?" she asked.

He threw back his head and laughed. "Not on your life. It's all good, Callie. It's all going to be good."

It's all going to be good.

She wished she could believe that. A lifetime of bad

outcomes had trained her to expect the worst. That was why she called Grant the next morning and told him she couldn't do it.

"I'll be right over," he said.

"No," she countered quickly. "It's no use. I'm going out. You can't change my mind."

"Why, Callie?"

She drew in a deep breath and sighed. "There is one big fat obstacle we didn't cover, and the more I think about it, the more I think it will doom our plans, no matter how careful we are."

"And that is…?"

"Love."

"Love?" His voice was hoarse. "I thought we'd settled that. We're against it."

"It's all very well to say this is totally a business deal, based on mutual benefits and ruled by facts and logic. But once we're married, we'll be together a lot. What if one of us loses our objectivity and…" She searched for the right words. "How are we going to guarantee we can keep this on a business level?"

He was silent for a moment. "That's a tricky one, I'll admit. In order to do this at all we have to have a certain affection for each other. We have to like each other."

"And I think we do," she said almost reluctantly.

"Absolutely. But neither of us wants any emotional entanglement. You don't want a reprise of your marriage, do you?"

"Heaven forbid." She sighed. If only he knew how

bad that had been. "But, Grant, there's still the danger of—well, one of us starting to care too much."

"I can tell you right now that this is not going to be a real problem for me," he said.

He paused and she could almost hear him weighing what he could tell her with what was just too much to reveal.

"I don't know how much you know about my marriage. Jan was the love of my life. The moment I met her I knew that she was the woman for me—and that was going to be forever." His voice lowered a bit, as though he was fighting off emotion. "I'm a forever kind of guy. We had our ups and downs, but she was my heartbeat." His voice sounded choked and he paused, steadying himself. "When I lost her and my little girl, I lost my life."

Callie closed her eyes for a few seconds. His pain was hard to bear.

"But my grandfather needed me," he said, going on after a pause to center himself. "I couldn't hurt him, he'd had enough grief in his life. And little by little, I pulled myself back out of the darkness."

His voice was gruff. This was obviously difficult for him to talk about. "I don't usually spill my guts this way, but I feel like we have to be honest. This is a big decision. I don't want to fall in love again. I've done that once. I just want to move on."

She nodded, though she knew he couldn't see her. She could hear the sincerity in his voice and she believed him.

"At the same time, I have this deep, hungry need for a child. I can't really explain it. It's partly that my grandfather would so love to see an heir in the pipeline. That would make up for a lot with him. But there's more to it. Maybe it's something embedded in my DNA. I don't know. But I need to have a child."

"I know," she whispered. "I feel the same way."

He was silent for a long moment, letting their agreement on the most important aspect sink in.

"Callie," he said at last. "Please give this more thought. I'm begging you."

She didn't answer him and he paused for a moment, then added, "I'll see you tomorrow night. Okay?"

"Okay," she said softly. And listened as he hung up.

Callie did give it more thought. The morning sun brought back her optimism and things didn't look so black and white. The entire project looked possible again.

And more thought brought up another issue. For all she knew, this might be her only chance. After all, she was almost thirty. There were no other prospective husbands on the horizon. Maybe this was just what she needed. All she had to do was throw caution to the wind.

Well, if that was all!

She was going to do it. She was going to marry Grant Carver and try to have a baby with him.

"It's a business arrangement," she told Tina, who took the news with openmouthed surprise. "It's not a love match."

Tina had the audacity to laugh at her for that pathetic proclamation.

"Right. There's no way in the world you could fall for a man like that. No way." She nodded wisely, then collapsed in giggles.

But Callie was determined to stand firm. After all, she'd been married before. She knew the ropes. Sort of.

Grant picked her up right on time and they cruised to the Cattlemen's Club for dinner. He didn't ask for her decision until they were seated at a round booth on a platform high enough to see out over the Dallas lights. They sat very close together this time, instead of across a table from each other. A sommelier poured out ruby-red wine in their crystal glasses, and Grant made a toast.

"To wedding bells and the pitter-patter of little feet," he said, smiling at her. "Will you drink to that, Callie Stevens?"

She knew exactly what he was asking. She met his gaze and felt a tingle. Here it was. Taking a deep breath, she nodded and held up her glass.

"Yes, Grant Carver," she said. "I'll drink to that, and what's more—I'll marry you."

The joy that leaped in his eyes made her breath catch in her throat and her heart start to thump. It was nice to be wanted—even if it was just a business deal. For just a moment, she thought he was going to toss aside his glass and take her in his arms and kiss her. She was ready to say no and to push him away, but her heart was beating even harder and she knew, no matter how hard she tried, she was not going to be able to avoid feeling a certain excitement when it came to being near this man.

She didn't have to do any jujitsu to keep him away. He controlled himself, but his smile wrapped around her almost as warmly as his arms would have.

"Brilliant," he said softly, his blue eyes shining. "You've made the right choice. Callie, we're going to make a great couple, you and I."

That would be lovely. She only hoped it was true. They sat very close and their heads got closer and they talked together almost like lovers, lost in a world of their own. Salads were served, and then the entrées, grilled duck for her, grilled steak for him. The food was delicious, the music from a string quartet romantic, the clinking of crystal and sterling silver a fine backdrop to the murmur of voices all around. Callie felt as though she'd stepped into a charmed land, a parallel universe, where good things just might happen after all.

"Well," she said at last. "When are we going to do it?"

"Tie the proverbial knot?" He smiled at her. "I've arranged for a marriage to be performed by a justice of the peace I know at his chambers next Wednesday. Subject to your approval, of course. That will give us time to clear up all the paperwork. We should bring along two witnesses. I'll bring my sister, Gena."

She nodded. "I'll bring Tina."

He paused and a shadow passed over his face, surprising her.

"Are you two really that close?" he asked.

"Oh, yes. We've known each other forever." She hesitated, then decided he might as well know the truth. "You see, we both had single mothers who died when we were teenagers, and no other family to go to. So we met when Social Services moved us into a group home with about ten other kids."

He stared at her, astounded. "Callie, I had no idea. My God, what you've been through!"

She meant to give him a reassuring smile, but she could tell it was coming off a bit tremulous.

"It was pretty ghastly at first. But once Tina and I found each other, it was like we formed a little family of our own. It made the whole experience bearable."

"So Tina is about as close to you as my sister is to me," he said, looking resigned.

She nodded. "I would do just about anything for her."

He looked troubled for a moment, and she wasn't sure why that should be. But he shook it off quickly enough as dessert arrived. Bananas Foster for them to share— set on fire by the waiter to caramelize the brown sugar.

"Oh, this is heavenly," Callie said. "I could live on this."

Grant didn't answer and she looked up to see why. He was watching her eat with a strange look on his face. Feeling slightly uncomfortable, she quickly brought up a new subject.

"I guess we ought to get some of the details settled," she said.

"Right," he said, nodding slowly. "I'm assuming my penthouse apartment will do until the baby comes. Of course, if you'd like to come over and see it so you can plan to move in right after the wedding…"

She stared at him, surprised. "Oh, do I really need to do that? I thought I would just stay where I am now until…"

"Callie, we're going to be married. Married people live together."

He was right, of course. She felt a little silly. She hadn't thought that through. Naturally they had to make this look as much as possible like a real marriage. What was she thinking?

"I guess you're right. But I'll have my own room."

He frowned. "If that's the way you want it," he said grudgingly.

She was surprised it was even an issue. "I think that would be best."

He shrugged, then thought of something that lifted his spirits.

"I've got a gift for you," he said, reaching into his pocket. "Close your eyes."

"What is it?"

"A surprise. Close your eyes."

She did so and felt him putting something on her finger.

"And now, we're officially engaged," he said.

Opening her eyes, she gasped at the beautiful ring he'd put on her hand. "Oh my goodness! Oh, it's beautiful!"

The diamond had to be over a carat, surrounded by smaller diamonds that sparkled with cool, crisp fire.

"Oh, Grant!"

"It was my mother's."

She froze, then turned slowly to face him.

"I can't take your mother's ring. Not for a business deal."

His eyes seemed to glow in the candlelight.

"Don't worry," he said with a twisted smile. "I've got a clause in the contract. If we divorce, you'll have to give it back."

"But Grant…."

"My mother passed away almost a year ago. She would have liked you. I'm sure she would approve."

She didn't know what to say. Somehow, this just wasn't right. His mother's ring—what if she lost it? But she could see that he wasn't going to listen to argument tonight. She would save that talk for later.

"It's wonderful, Grant. Thank you so much."

He smiled. He was so close, she could feel him as well as see him. He was going to kiss her now. She could sense it. And this time, she thought she might just let him. She smiled and looked at his beautiful mouth and waited, heart beating. But he didn't come any closer. And suddenly he was talking about garage parking places and getting her a key to his apartment and all the other details of everyday life they were going to have to adjust to.

She hardly heard him. She'd been so sure he was going to kiss her. It wouldn't have been much of a kiss, of course. This wasn't the place for passion—and anyway, passion wasn't supposed to be a part of their relationship, she added to herself hastily. But a soft kiss to seal the deal would have been appropriate. Wouldn't it? She'd been so ready. Surely he'd seen how she'd tilted her face to accept him. And yet, he'd held back.

She would have liked to blame it on his mouth still being sore from the stitches. Maybe that was it. But somehow, she doubted it.

Bottom line, did he feel anything for her at all?

Hold on there, Callie, she told herself briskly. He wasn't supposed to feel anything. Remember?

This is not a love match. This is pure business.

Okay. Then that was the way she was going to treat it. Even if she fell in love with him.

Deep inside, she groaned. Where had that thought come from? From her darkest fears, no doubt. She'd been telling herself for years that she didn't have the knack for falling in love. She'd come in contact with a lot of attractive men and felt nothing. She didn't expect to fall for Grant. But what if she did? Was she crazy to risk it this way?

Maybe. But she'd made her decision and she was going to stand by it. A lot was riding on success here.

"Should we decide on a doctor?" she asked when he'd stopped talking for a moment.

He looked surprised. "Don't you have an ob/gyn?"

"Of course, for the pregnancy. But who are we going to use for the… You know." She gave a small shrug, surprised to find herself embarrassed.

But he frowned, looking at her as though he couldn't believe what he was hearing.

"No, I don't know. What are you talking about?"

She couldn't imagine why he was being so obtuse. What had he been talking about all this time, anyway? He was the one who'd wanted to do this first.

"Well, we're going to need to be tested," she reminded him, trying to be as delicate as she could. But it wasn't easy with a subject like this. "And you're going to need to…make a deposit and…"

"Wait a minute." He stared at her, thunderstruck. "You thought we were still going to use artificial insemination?"

She blinked at him. "Why yes. I thought…"

"Callie!" He laughed a big, booming laugh that rolled across the room and turned heads. "I think we're perfectly capable of doing this on our own. Don't you?"

She wanted to put a hand over his mouth and quiet him down. The whole room was listening. And here was Grant, saying…

"On our own?" She gazed at him, puzzled. "Oh, you mean…"

"Of course. That's what I mean. You and me. Together."

He stared at her, suddenly realizing she was serious. It hadn't occurred to him that she would still be thinking along those lines. He was going to have to step lightly here.

"It's up to you, of course. But I think we can manage something a little bit more personal, don't you?"

She bit her lip. Her heart was thumping. She hadn't realized… But of course he was right. One of the things that had turned her away from artificial insemination had been the cold, clinical nature of the process—not to mention the prospect of all those doctor's visits.

"After all," he was saying, "we've both been married before. We're both sexually experienced. Aren't we?"

"Actually…" She looked down at where her hands were curved around a coffee cup and turned beet-red.

"You're kidding." He didn't know what to say. "You were married, right?"

"Yes, but…" She looked up at him, her dark eyes filled with a confusion that touched him in a way he hadn't expected at all. "He couldn't… He didn't…"

How could she explain her marriage to a man who seemed to think of her as a sort of doll, a prized possession rather than a flesh and blood woman? His lack of interest in marital relations had confused her from the beginning and she still didn't really understand it herself.

"You poor kid." He wanted to pull her into his arms and hold her tightly, but this was too public a place for that. Instead he touched her cheek lightly. "Callie, don't worry. We won't do anything until you're ready."

Her smile seemed a bit tremulous at first, then she appeared to regain her equilibrium and it broadened.

"Same here," she told him, a mischievous light in her eyes. "I won't push you into anything you're not ready for, either."

He grinned. "Don't worry about me. I'm ready right now."

She laughed, but he wasn't joking. Watching her, with her beautiful face and her silken skin, and that hair that fell around her shoulders like a symphony come to life, he knew he was more than ready. He wanted her in a deep, aching way that was going to be a problem if he didn't watch out. But something told him it would be a problem he could live with.

CHAPTER FIVE

WHITE lace and promises.

What a picture those words conjured up—every girl's dream. Callie had always loved weddings, the more white lace the better. But she hadn't loved her first wedding much. Stark and quick, it had been kind of strange. She was beginning to worry that her second wedding wasn't going to be any better. She was going to have two weddings under her belt and neither one of them traditional. Oh well, maybe she just wasn't meant to be a traditional girl.

Grant had made the arrangements and from what he'd told her, the prospects were good this one was going to be as spare and unromantic as the first one had been—a utilitarian ceremony in a government office somewhere with just two witnesses. It sounded a lot like getting a driver's license. She'd been dreading it the way she dreaded a trip to the dentist—something unpleasant that had to be done in order to get on with life. Nothing to look forward to at all.

She'd been working at the office all week and she liked her new job. She even liked seeing Grant across the room every now and then. The people she worked with had oohed and aahed over her engagement ring, but she'd managed to keep the name of the groom mysterious. It was going to be an awkward moment when she finally revealed that she was marrying the boss. Oh well. Just another of life's little bumps in the road.

Grant had taken her to dinner a few nights into the week, and his sister had joined them. Gena was tall and slender and just as attractive as her brother was. They both had the look of Texas aristocracy—people whose ancestors had ridden through the purple sage and fought off attackers and run cattle across the land and built this state into what it was today.

And here she was marrying into that legacy and expected to produce an heir with those bloodlines. When you thought about it that way, it was quite a responsibility. Maybe she should feel honored. Somehow, she didn't.

"Will your grandfather be at the wedding?" she'd asked Grant. She knew that both his parents had died, but that his grandfather was still very much a part of his life and active in Texas affairs.

"No. His mind is still sharp as a tack, but he can't get around very well any longer and it would be too hard on him to cart him over for the wedding. We'll pay him a visit instead."

He took her to meet the older man the next day. Grant

Carver IV lived about half an hour out of town on the Lazy Drifter Ranch that had been in Carver hands for about a hundred and fifty years. A dignified, elegantly aging man, he terrified her at first, looking her over narrowly and peppering her with questions. But after a few minutes, he warmed to her and by the time they excused themselves so that Grant could give Callie a tour of the ranch, he'd given her a hug and given both of them his blessing.

"I like him," she said as they walked through the huge foyer of the ranch house. "Do you suppose you'll look just like that when you're in your eighties?" She gave him a teasing smile. "After all, you're the sixth edition of the Grant Carver icon." Her smile faded as she remembered what that meant. "And I'm supposed to produce the seventh, aren't I?"

"That's the plan," he admitted. "Having second thoughts?"

She looked around at the beautiful house, the spacious vistas out across the huge ranch, the modern equipment juxtaposed with working cowboys on horses, and finally, at the man himself.

Second thoughts? Sure. Plans to back out? No. After all, she'd bought into a life most women could only dream of. Whether it would turn out to be her dream—or her nightmare—only time would tell. But the old saying came to mind, nothing ventured, nothing gained. She was taking chances, but she was ready for them.

She smiled at Grant. "Ready or not," she said in answer to his question, "I'm here for the party."

"Good."

She liked the way he looked here in his family home. She'd worn white slacks and a soft blue shirt with a white scarf at her neck and she'd thought that would look country.

But Grant was the real deal. His boots looked like they'd been worn at the Alamo, his jeans were scuffed almost threadbare in places and held up by a wide leather belt sporting a huge brass belt buckle with a big rattlesnake worked into the metal. His cotton shirt was open at the neck, displaying some gorgeous flesh. The sleeves were pushed back, revealing muscular forearms. All in all, he was the picture of what a fantasy cowboy would look like. It made her gasp a little every time she looked at him.

She met Misty, the family dog, a golden retriever with a permanent grin and a mischievous glint in her eyes. Then Grant introduced her to Rosa Cortez, the woman who had been housekeeper at the ranch, "since time began," as he put it. A plump, chatty woman, she promised to fix them a nice lunch for later in the day. Taking Misty along with them, they made their way outside and he led her to the barn and then to the stables, where Callie touched a horse for the first time in her life.

"They are so big!" she cried, awed and a little nervous at the same time. "They don't seem that big in the movies."

"I can't believe you've never been riding," Grant said, shaking his head. "We'll have to remedy that real soon. We'll get you up on ol' Bessie there. She's gentle as a kitten. You'll love it."

Callie stroked Bessie's nose and looked into her deep, soft eyes. She liked Bessie just fine, but she didn't think she was going to relish riding her. "I've always liked having both feet on the ground," she said. "I don't really see any reason to give that up."

He laughed. "You just wait. Once you get used to horses and we let you go, you'll feel like you're flying."

She didn't bother to quibble aloud, but she had no intention of ever getting up on a horse. Still, she had to admit they were beautiful and she loved their eyelashes. Following Grant through to the opposite doorway, she stopped and spoke to each horse she found. Some snickered back, some ignored her. But she didn't want anyone to feel left out.

Out behind the stables was a corral where a number of cowboys had gathered. As she and Grant approached, Callie could see that they were working with large calves and from the smell of burned hair, she realized they were probably branding them. She wrinkled her nose, not sure she was going to enjoy this much. She glanced at Grant, thinking to suggest going on back to the house, but then she noticed the look on his face and she turned quickly to see who he was looking at.

A tall, handsome cowboy wearing leather chaps detached from the others and came toward them. The two men stopped in a squared-off fashion and grinned at each other.

"Hey," said Grant, touching the brim of his hat.

"Hey," said the cowboy, touching his as well.

That was it, but she could tell these two men were old, close friends. In California, they would have hugged. In France, they would have been kissing cheeks. But this was Texas—old Texas. And she liked it.

"Callie, meet Will Jamison."

She smiled and he touched his hat again and said, "Nice to meet you, Callie."

"Will's the ranch foreman. Just like his daddy was before him." Grant nodded. "He and I go way back."

"Back so far," Will agreed, "I sometimes wonder if we weren't switched at birth. Maybe *I* should be the one riding around in that fancy car and you should be the one working here, eatin' dirt all day."

"Pay him no mind, Callie," Grant advised her. "He's just aiming to play on your sympathies." He grinned. "Just try to get this man into a suit and tie for even one day. He'd come running back to the ranch so fast."

"We were raised together," Will told her in a friendly manner, bending down to scratch Misty behind the ears. "Two peas in a pod. Until he had to ruin everything by going off to become a city slicker."

"Hey, man's gotta work for a livin'."

Will snorted. "You call that sissy stuff you do in the city working? I'll show you working." He reached for a coil of rope he had slung over his shoulder. "Here, let's see if you've still got the touch."

Grant took the rope, looking at it almost lovingly.

"Let's see you bring in one of those young ones," Will said, gesturing toward where the work was going on. "And lay our brand right on his backside."

Grant tried his hand with the rope, twisting it and twirling it a bit. "Man, I haven't done this for years and years," he said, pulling up one end and starting a slipknot.

"Well, never mind then," Will teased. "I wouldn't want to mess up those soft, lily-white hands of yours with some real man's work."

"Stand back, cowboy," Grant drawled, his lasso in his hand. "I got me some ropin' to do."

He set off toward where the calves were being released with a Western swagger that was only partly facetious.

Will grinned and winked at Callie. "Come on over here, Callie," he said, leading the way to a good vantage point against the railings. "You don't want to miss this."

Grant did pretty well, actually. Will kept up a running commentary, mostly for Callie's sake, but also to poke fun at Grant occasionally. Watching Grant hog-tie a big, rough-looking calf made Callie wince and bite her lip, and when he reached for the red-hot branding iron, she had to close her eyes and groan a little.

Will looked at her curiously. "You from Texas?" he asked skeptically.

"Yes, I'm from Texas." She tossed her hair back and raised her chin proudly. "Born and raised."

"In Dallas, I'm thinkin'," he said, shaking his head as though it were a darn shame.

"That's true. I'm city raised." And then she added something she'd never told anyone before. "But I'm told my daddy was a rodeo champion. A bronc buster."

Will's face changed. "No kidding. What was his name?"

She shrugged. "He didn't stick around long enough to give me his name. My mother told me once and I wrote it down somewhere. I suppose I could find it if a real need arose."

"I see." Will's gaze darkened a bit. "One of those drive-by parenting situations, huh?"

"You got it."

They were quiet for a moment, watching Grant. He was working hard and doing quite a bit of shouting, it seemed to Callie. Misty was bouncing around, trying to help, and barking whenever Grant shouted, as though to back him up. But he looked to be in his element. Who would have thought she'd be marrying a cowboy? That made her smile.

As the newly branded calf ran off to get away from these crazy ranchers, Will turned to her again.

"So I hear you and Grant are fixin' to get hitched," he said, giving her a searching look.

She nodded. "You heard right."

"You couldn't get a better man. He'll do you proud. Don't you doubt it."

She heard the sincerity in his voice and saw it in his

eyes. "You know," she said softly, "I think you just may be right."

He nodded. "But we're going to have to teach you how to ride and how to be a ranch wife."

She tried to smile but couldn't quite make it. "Do I have to?"

"Sure. You're going to be a Carver. You gotta know your way around ranching."

Hold it just a minute there.

This wasn't what she'd signed on for. She gazed at him, a little worried.

"Did Jan do it?" she asked, and the moment the words left her lips she wished she could pull them back. This was none of her business. Why was Jan on her mind so often?

But Will didn't seem bothered by the question.

"No, as a matter of fact, she did not. And believe me, that was a problem now and then." He looked as though he was about to launch into a fuller explanation, but he caught himself and stopped, staring at her.

"To me, you look like a smarter gal," he said instead. "I think you probably understand that compromises must be made in all parts of life, even when wrasslin' cattle. One person can't always be the one to win. You got to develop an instinct for where to give in and where to stand firm. Just like Grant's been doing out there right now."

Grant called to him and he responded in kind, but Callie stayed where she was, thinking over what he'd said. One thing she hadn't expected was a lesson in life from a cowboy. But she had to admit, Will had a few home truths to convey. She was glad he seemed to take to her. He might be an important ally in the future.

Grant came back to her looking a bit worse for wear, but very pleased with himself.

"I can still hold my own," he proclaimed proudly. "Hell, I could come back here and take over running this ranch and have it doing twice as good as it's doing now."

That last was for Will's benefit, and they argued good-naturedly for a moment or two. Grant slung an arm around Callie's shoulders and began to lead her back to the house, still ragging on his friend. But when Callie glanced back, she caught Will giving Grant a thumbs-up that was obviously meant to convey approval of his marriage choice. That gave her a glow that matched the one Grant was riding on.

Back in the house, Grant washed up while Callie wandered around, admiring the rustic but strangely elegant furnishings. He came out looking freshly scrubbed.

"Rosa says she'll lay lunch out in half an hour," he told her.

"What will we do until then?"

He thought for a moment, then had an idea.

"Come on," he said with a lascivious wink that was pure mockery. "I'll take you up to my bedroom."

CHAPTER SIX

FEIGNED suspicion filled Callie's dark eyes and she dug in her heels.

"Why?" she demanded to know.

Grant grinned and tugged on her hand. "Just to show you."

She frowned. "Show me what?"

"I don't know. All my trophies. How's that?" He laughed. "Come on. Follow me."

She wasn't seriously reluctant, so she did follow him and they ended up in a large room overlooking the back garden. A huge bed took up most of the middle of the room.

"Wow. This bed looks big enough to have a party in," she said.

She colored when he laughed and she realized how that could be taken.

"Too bad I was such a shy guy I never thought of that myself," he said sadly.

She threw him a skeptical look. "Shy guy" just

didn't fit with the man she was getting to know. "Right."

Lowering herself to sit on the edge of the bed, she looked around at the furnishings. Basketballs, baseball gloves, a snowboard, a racing bike, trophies and banners. There was no doubt this room had belonged to a male child. She had a quick vision of all the friends and fantasies that must have passed through this room over the years.

"You know, this is just crazy," she said softly, looking up at him. "How can I marry you? I don't really know you. I don't know what sort of person you really are." She studied him, frowning. "I don't know if you've been a solid citizen or a womanizer. I don't know if you cheat on your taxes or…or rescue little donkeys from the snow. Who are you?"

He stared at her for a moment. "It doesn't usually snow in this part of Texas," he said at last. "At least not when the donkeys are out."

She bit her lip. She refused to laugh. Instead she rose and began wandering about the room, looking at the artifacts of his growing up years.

"Tell me something I don't know," she said, picking up an endearing picture of a young Grant in a soccer uniform. He was trying to look tough and fierce for the camera. "Tell me what you were like as a child," she said, setting it down.

"As a child?" His shrug was nonchalant. "I was a boy genius, of course."

"Really." She perused the titles in his bookcase—mostly old textbooks. "Tell me more."

"Well, let's see." He struck a pose as though harkening back in time. "Naturally I was a Boy Scout. Helped my share of old ladies across the street. Won all my badges."

"What else?" she asked, assuming he was only half-serious. There was a mocking tone to his attitude that let her know he wasn't going to reveal any more than he had to.

"There's not much more."

She gave him a look. "Come on. Make an effort. I need to know."

He shrugged and his voice took on the timbre of a radio announcer.

"I was a studious lad right from the start. Top honors in recitation. Walked miles through the snow to get to school."

"I thought you just said it didn't snow around here."

"Snow in the metaphorical sense, of course."

She sighed, losing hope of getting anything honest out of him now. "I should have known."

He went on. "When I wasn't studying, I was collecting things. Coins, stamps, butterflies."

"Girlfriends?" she suggested casually, finding a stack of annuals and taking one up to flip through.

He scowled at her. "Never."

"No kidding." She raised an eyebrow as she found a page in his annual signed by lots of girlish sounding names.

"Of course. I was the model student. Summers I spent at science camp. I wrote journals and was president of the entomology club. Advisor to Student Scholars. Champion at one-hour chess. I had no time for frivolous things like girls and parties and…"

"Hmm. Then I guess this yearbook must belong to some other guy named Grant. Here's a note from someone named Snookie. 'My dearest Grant,'" she read from the page, glancing up to see how he was taking it. "'Thanks so much for giving me your picture. I keep it under my pillow so I can kiss you good-night every night. I pretend I'm your one and only girl, even though you explained to me how you don't believe in going steady…'" She looked up at him, aghast. "You cad!" she cried.

He shrugged and tried to look innocent. "Snookie? Never heard of her."

"Here's another one. 'Grant, you hottie! I saved you a seat in assembly but you didn't show up. I'm looking forward to Friday night. You are so hot! Love, Mimi.'"

Grant's innocent act was beginning to fray around the edges and he was looking a little shifty-eyed.

"I don't remember any Mimi, either," he said before she had a chance to make a comment.

"I'll bet she remembers you."

He frowned, shoved his hands down deep into his pockets and looked at her sideways, trying a new direction. "You know, I really think this is a sad case of mistaken identity."

"Really?"

He nodded hopefully. "It's like you said. She must have meant some other Grant."

"Right." She nodded, eyes dancing. "I'll bet your school was just brimming with guys named Grant Carver."

He grimaced. "Brimming with Grant Carver wannabes, maybe," he muttered.

She grinned. "Okay, let's see if we can pin this down," she said, turning to the index. "This Grant Carver was captain of the swim team. King of Junior Prom. Senior class president. Does that ring a bell?"

He blinked blankly and shrugged. "Who remembers high school?"

"Oh, wait! This Grant Carver was voted 'Most Likely To Be Shot By A Jealous Husband.'" She looked up, her eyes dancing at his discomfort. "Grant, I don't see anything about the chess club here."

"They must have left that out." He grimaced. "Never mind. Let's go down and see if lunch is ready."

She shook her head. "Let's read more of those letters."

"Let's not." He made a halfhearted pass at grabbing the book from her but she kicked off her shoes and jumped up on the bed, out of reach.

"'Dear Grant,'" she read. "'You are so cool, but your kiss is so hot.'" She laughed. "All these references to heat. A theme seems to be coming through, don't you think? Hot, hot, hot." She made a face at him.

His eyes were smiling but he was pretending to frown and tried to grab the book again. "Give me that."

"No!" she cried, bouncing away from his reach. "We

must read all the letters. The truth must come out! Your wild past can't be suppressed forever." She frowned down at him. "Was this really your attitude toward girls in those days? Sexist pig."

"I told you. That isn't me."

"Then who is it, your evil twin?"

"Could be. I won't know until you hand over the book."

"Hah!"

He held out his hand. "Give me the book."

She taunted him with a grin. "Make me."

He didn't hesitate. In one bound, he was up on the bed with her. Laughing, she tried to get away, and when that didn't work, she clung to the yearbook, trying to keep him from taking it. That didn't last long. He had the book, and then she was falling onto the soft surface of the bed and he was falling with her.

They landed together, face-to-face, her hands flattened on his chest. She was still laughing, but when she looked into his eyes, she saw something darker and more disturbed there.

"Hi," she said softly.

He couldn't answer her. He was too busy trying not to want her.

His hands were clutched in fists to keep from touching her. And because this was so hard, he had to ask himself—could he do this? Could he marry another woman? He stared down into Callie's dark eyes and searched for an answer.

Callie's face had a look of impatience, as though

she'd waited for something that hadn't happened and she was getting darn tired of this. With a flash of quick irritation, she threw her arms around his neck.

"If you can't even kiss me, how are we ever going to make love?" she whispered.

He stared down at her. She didn't understand. Sex was just sex. He could do that anytime, anywhere. But kissing—that was opening up and letting someone in—a connection between heart and soul. Once he'd kissed her…

She was giving up. Her hands slid down from his neck and a hurt look filled her eyes. He couldn't stand that, and without letting himself think, he lowered his mouth to hers.

Hot buttered rum. That was what she tasted like. Smooth and creamy and slightly intoxicating. And addictive. Once the kiss started, he wasn't sure he was going to be able to stop it. She was so soft, so sweet… Desire rose in him like a sort of madness, threatening to take away his ability to reason.

As he struggled to pull away, the thoughts came anyway, fast and confusing. He didn't want to feel this sort of urgency, this need to take her in his arms. But it had been so long since he'd held a woman and his body wanted hers so badly. At the same time, he had to hold himself back. He wasn't free to do what came naturally. He had to remember…

"I'm sorry," she was saying.

He looked down, startled. Her gaze was still troubled.

"I shouldn't have pushed you into that," she said. "I know you didn't want to do it."

His mind was still too thick to process coherent thoughts. Pulling back away from her, he rose on his elbow and watched her for a moment.

"This isn't going to be easy for either of us," he said at last. "What we're planning to do will go against all our basic instincts."

She nodded. "I know."

Rolling over, she sat on the edge of the bed and looked back at him. She was reeling from that kiss, but working hard to keep that information close to the vest. But, oh my! Her lips were still vibrating. She'd never been kissed like that before. In fact, she didn't know it could be that way. And worst of all, she was dying to feel that way again.

Should she tell him? Should she warn him that she might not be able to keep the sort of distance they were planning to maintain in their marriage? Maybe she should let him know. He had a right to that information.

But before she had a chance to say anything more, Rosa called from the stairs, letting them know that lunch was getting cold. They both rose from the bed, pulled their clothing together and started down to the lunch-room. And Callie let that moment slip away.

The lunch was delicious—tortilla soup and taco salad. As they ate, they both seemed to gradually lose the edgy sensitivity they'd picked up on that bed, and before long, they were talking and kidding again, instead of feeling that strange sensual connection.

"So tell me," Callie said as they started on their bowls of ice cream for dessert. "On the level. What is the truth about you?"

"About me?" He shrugged as though it hardly mattered. "Hard to say. It's probably about halfway in between what you were thinking and what I was saying."

"Oh." She thought for a few seconds. "Well, I guess that's helpful. In a way."

"Okay, here's the real truth," he began, waving his spoon at her.

"As opposed to the unreal truth you've been telling me so far?" she teased.

Giving her a superior look, he ignored her comment and went on.

"Unfortunately it's a very boring story. I had good parents, a great sister, friends and extended family. I did well in school, but I wasn't the best. I got into a good college and did well there. I met a wonderful girl…."

His voice suddenly seemed to fail him. He'd meant to go on and tell her about Jan, she was sure, but right now, he just couldn't do it.

"Anyway, just a normal American upbringing," he said instead, avoiding her gaze as he put his napkin on the table.

"Sure," she said, trying to sound casual after an awkward moment of silence. "With a little more money than most, a little more background, a huge Texas ranch and a major business in the family. Let's face it, Grant. You are one of the blessed."

He nodded slowly. "Yes. You're right. I had a lot of advantages. And I'm grateful." His voice got rougher as he added, "But I'd give it all up if I could change a few things."

With a nod to her, he rose and walked out of the room, leaving it at that.

Callie looked around the room and wondered how often Jan had been here with him. It was obvious he was feeling the emptiness she'd left behind right now—that he was fighting off heartbreak. She wished she knew how to help him, but she was afraid that was a wound that just wasn't going to heal.

Could she live with that? She was going to have to. Either that, or back out of this project. Because Jan was going to be the third member of their marriage, from what she could see. And she couldn't say he hadn't warned her.

The next day, Callie took her lunch hour to go to see her mother-in-law from her first marriage. Marge Stevens lived in a twilight doze most of the time, but she always brightened when she realized it was Callie leaning down to give her a kiss on her withered cheek. Thanks to Grant, she was in a better nursing home situation now, being cared for every minute by loving attendants.

Still, Callie thought how lucky Grant's grandfather was to still be well enough to be living at home, even if he wasn't very mobile any longer. It was just too bad he couldn't see the wedding he was so interested in having take place.

And then, she had an idea. She stopped by Grant's office when she got back to work.

"Grant, I know your grandfather can't come into town for our wedding. But listen. Why don't we take it to him? Why don't we have the justice come out to the ranch? Would he do that?"

Grant thought it was a great idea and she could see that he appreciated her thinking of his grandfather that way. She had a warm glow for the rest of the afternoon.

But in the end, it turned out she should have left well enough alone. The plan had been to have a quiet, private wedding in the justice's chambers with two witnesses. That was it, just a quick transaction, shake hands and off everyone would go. Instead, now that they were having the wedding at the ranch, everything was turned on its head.

She couldn't blame anybody but herself. It had been her idea. But once the setting changed, things started spiraling out of control, and before she knew it, she was being asked what sort of wedding cake she wanted and did she want to have finger food or a sit-down dinner, and did she mind if the cousins from Redmond came? They would stay quiet and in the background, but they were older and had loved Grant as though he were a child of their own and would be so hurt if they found out they hadn't been included.

So suddenly they were having the wedding of the year, out in ranch country at any rate. When everyone you met was just so excited about the wedding, how could you keep them away?

"I don't even have a decent dress to wear," Callie fretted as the whole thing loomed like a curse just a day away. "I mean, if we were really doing this right, I would have a hair appointment and a dress and veil and all the other things a bride expects to have. And here I am, going into a big wedding with little wedding outfits and preparations."

"I thought that was what you wanted," Tina said.

"Sometimes I want dumb things," she said, frowning her frustration. "I'm getting a very bad feeling about this. Is someone trying to tell me something? Is this a sign that I'm not prepared for this marriage? That I'm doing something recklessly without considering all the ramifications?"

"Oh, calm down," Tina said, trying to reassure her. "You've just got the jitters. Everything will be fine tomorrow. You'll see."

Callie tried to calm down. She took a long shower. She washed her hair. She packed a case of things she was planning to take out to the ranch to use in the wedding. Then she repacked the case she'd prepared to take to Grant's apartment after the wedding. Then she repacked it again. Then she put a new shade of polish on her toenails and redid her fingernails.

But the whole time, all she could think about was Grant. How could she marry a man who was still in love with his first wife?

She was getting married for the second time. Was this her second big mistake? She'd married Ralph, her first husband, because he and his mother had been good to her when she was desperate and she was grateful. And now—had she fallen into the same trap again? She was marrying Grant because he promised to take care of all her problems and make life smooth and easy for her. How was that so different from the reasons she'd used to talk herself into marrying Ralph, another man she didn't love?

Why couldn't she seem to learn from her mistakes? Was she one of these people who kept falling into the same pattern again and again and ruined their lives?

"It's different this time," she whispered to herself.

Yeah. Right. That was what those sorts of people always said, wasn't it?

"No, really. It's different. Because this time, I understand what I'm getting into. I'm not expecting marriage to make everything perfect."

Perfect? This might not even end up normally average, forget perfect.

She went back over all the steps in her head, reminding herself of how this was a business deal first and foremost. That they were both in this for something other than the usual love thing. That they both had to keep cool, calm and collected if this was going to work for them.

No emotions. At least, not so anyone would notice.

But she just wasn't sure if that was going to work in the long run. In fact, she was afraid she already liked

Grant a little too much. Should she tell him? If not, could she keep a secret like that for the rest of her life?

This was agony. Maybe they should just forget the whole thing. Maybe she ought to call him and...

It was late when Grant picked up the phone. He heard Tina's voice on the other end.

"You'd better get over here fast," she said.

He tensed. "What's wrong?"

"We've got a bad case of cold feet developing. You might want to come over and try to nip it in the bud."

Funny, but he'd been expecting this. In fact, he'd faced a bit of the old frigid feet thing himself, wondering how he could possibly be contemplating doing something so contrived and difficult to bring off.

"If you still want to marry this woman tomorrow," Tina was saying, "you'd better come and make your case."

"Again?"

"Again."

He sighed. But what the hell—maybe trying to convince her would firm up the crumbling edges of his own confidence.

"Okay," Tina was saying. "I'm going to take Molly and go grocery shopping. You will have about an hour and a half before I get back. Put it to good use."

Good old Tina. He'd gotten to know her better over the past week and understood why she and Callie were so close. He was glad she was on his side. If she were working against him, he wouldn't have a chance.

He was at the apartment in twenty minutes. Callie was home and she let him in, looking curious but not particularly surprised to see him.

"Tina called you, right?"

"She said your resolution was wilting. I came over to give it life support."

She gave him a tragic look, turned and led the way to the couch, where she flopped down, pulling her legs up under her. He sat down in a chair facing her and spent a moment enjoying the way the lamplight played with her golden hair.

"You're not going to desert me, are you?" he asked her softly.

She met his gaze and held it for a long moment before she slowly shook her head. "I don't think so," she said doubtfully.

He could have asked for a little more positive spin on that less-than-ringing endorsement. But at least she wasn't calling him names and throwing things.

"Tell me, Callie. What is it that's making you feel uncertain tonight?"

She closed her eyes, took a deep breath and opened them again.

"Oh, I don't know. This whole thing. I mean, this started out being a small business deal. Remember that? Now we're stuck with this gigantic wedding with all sorts of people coming, lots who I don't even know. This wasn't supposed to happen. It's all gotten out of hand."

"No, it hasn't," he said, leaning forward with his

elbows on his knees, all calm male confidence and optimism. "Callie, the wedding as a party means nothing. Officially joining our lives in the pursuit of a baby—that's what's important. All the rest is frills." He shrugged. "If you want, we'll cancel it and go back to our original plan."

She stared at him. "We can't do that."

"Why not?"

She bit her lip. "Everybody's so excited about it."

"Great." He smiled at her. "Let them have the party without us. We don't have to go."

She smiled, thinking of it. Most of them wouldn't notice the bride and groom were missing until halfway through the day. She could imagine the scene.

"Really?"

"Sure. It doesn't bother me."

She laughed softly, looking at him. Why was he being so nice and understanding?

Because he doesn't want to lose his chance at having his baby. Well, yes. That was true. Still, she liked that he didn't just come in shouting like some men she'd known.

"But it's not just the wedding is it?" he said.

Her smile faded. "No, not really. It's this whole strange situation we've gotten ourselves into. I'm not sure we're doing the right thing."

He nodded. "Is it your first husband? Do you feel as though you're betraying him in some way?" This was a scenario he knew only too well, so it was the first thing that came to mind.

"What?" She looked surprised at the suggestion. Betray Ralph? Hardly. "Oh, no. Not at all."

He was glad it wasn't that. Still, maybe there were deeper emotions here than she even realized herself. When you came right down to it, he didn't know much about the man she'd married before. And what he did know was baffling, to say the least.

"Why don't you tell me about him?"

"Ralph?" She wrinkled her nose. "Now?"

"Sure. We've got to do it sometime. Why don't we get it out of the way now? Tell me why you married Ralph."

She looked down at her hands, folded in her lap. Taking a breath deep into her lungs, she held it for a moment, let it out and looked up at Grant, smiling.

"Okay."

She settled back into the couch. "I told you that I spent many of my teenage years in a group home. You had to leave when you turned eighteen. Ready or not, out you went."

He nodded, his blue eyes dark in the shadows.

"Tina is a year younger than I am and she stayed on. But I had to go. I had to find a place for myself in the world. They gave us classes and counseling and all that, but you get such outlandish expectations when you're young. I thought I could do anything."

She smiled, remembering. "I was going to get a fabulous job and start college and find a boyfriend. It was all going to be wonderful. And when reality slapped me in the face and I couldn't get a job that would pay enough to let me rent a decent place and still have money left over for food, I felt very lost and cheated for a time. I really struggled."

It had been harder than she could express to him, harder than she would want to express to anyone. But it had helped make her into who she was today, she had to admit.

"And then, I saw an ad in the paper for an older woman who needed a paid companion. The job didn't pay much but it came with room and board and would give me time to start taking college classes."

She paused, smiling as she remembered. "Marge Stevens was…is…a wonderful person. She became a second mother to me in many ways. Without her, I don't know what would have happened to me.

"Ralph was her son. He was in his thirties at the time. A lot older than I was. A pleasant, good-looking man. He traveled a lot, but came home at least once a month to visit with his mother. She adored him. He seemed to adore me. He helped me and taught me a lot. One thing led to another, and before I knew it, I'd agreed to marry him."

"Just like that?"

She nodded, suppressing a smile. *Yes, Grant, just like that. Just the way I'm jumping into marrying you, too. See what an idiot I am? I just keep doing it.*

Sighing, she went on aloud. "They'd both been so good to me and they both wanted me to do it so badly. I sort of felt like I owed them. If it hadn't been for Marge, I would never have been able to get through as much college as I did. She helped me a lot. And at the same time, Ralph seemed very ardent and I thought maybe this was love, for me, too."

"Naive," he muttered.

She leaned forward earnestly. "Listen, try to understand. Ralph was pretty much the first man who'd been good to me. My experience with men over the first decades of my life hadn't been real positive. First there were my mother's boyfriends who came and went and treated her horribly when they weren't trying to hit on her little girl behind her back."

She paused for a moment, swallowing hard. She'd never hinted at that before to anyone but Tina, and now here she'd casually told Grant. She looked at his eyes, but she didn't see condemnation. Squaring her shoulders, she went on.

"Then there were the administrators of the group home. One man in particular enjoyed making sure we understood how worthless we were and how much we owed to him and his staff for all we got. And finally, the few guys I dated in college all turned out to be jerks. So when Ralph treated me as an equal, as someone worth talking to, I was just so happy to find a man like that, it helped to win me over."

His eyes flashed and she wasn't sure if it was with anger or something else.

"And you regretted it?" he asked, his voice rough.

"Oh, yes. I definitely regretted it. Not that Ralph ever did anything horrible to me. Not physically. But once we were married, that sweet, considerate man turned into a control freak suspicious of everything I did and everyone I talked to. He couldn't let me go to the grocery store alone. He was sure I was seeing someone behind his back. It was crazy."

"Hmm. What did he do for a living?"

"He was a sort of freelance photojournalist. Every now and then he actually sold a picture. But mostly, he lived off his mother's tiny nest egg and her social security."

"Great guy."

She bit her lip. Funny, but she had an impulse to defend Ralph. He wasn't much, but he'd been hers for a time. Still, she resisted it.

"He drank too much, of course, and finally he got drunk and fell in the street and hit his head just wrong. He was dead in three days."

She reached into her pocket for a band and pulled her hair into a ponytail, tying it back. "It was sad, especially for Marge. But we never had a real marriage."

He nodded, glad they had done this. He thought he'd found out what he needed to know—that she didn't have any deep emotional ties to the man. They could pretty much close that chapter of her life.

But that left what he knew was unspoken between them—the real concern. How was this going to work with him still attached to Jan? Was he going to be able to give Callie what she needed when he was still held hostage to the past?

And what about Callie—could she ever give up on

finding real love herself? Was it all worth it? Seemingly she'd made that decision and decided it was worth it. Was she regretting it? He didn't really think so. Worried, maybe, but not regretting it. He hoped she would feel free to tell him what she was thinking.

"Let's promise one thing to each other right now," he said. "We'll always be honest with each other. We can't deal with a problem if we don't know what it is."

She nodded. She agreed. Sure, she would try to be honest. Later.

He wanted to fix things, make everything okay. But if she started being honest right now, she would have to tell him, "Grant, I'm scared to marry you because I'm so afraid I'm going to fall in love with you, and I know your heart is unavailable." How was he going to fix that?

She couldn't be that honest because she was in too deep. And she couldn't pull away now.

"Don't worry," she said aloud to him instead. "I'm going to marry you tomorrow. There are just a few emotional hurdles I have to leap over first. I'll get there."

He nodded, looking troubled. "Get some sleep. I'll pick you up early tomorrow and we'll head out to the ranch."

"Okay."

He looked at her for a long moment, then turned away. "Good night," he said.

"Good night," she echoed, feeling a bit abandoned.

He reached the door and paused, then looked back at her. She was standing under the light in the entryway. She'd tied her hair back but strands were escaping all around her face, making her look like an angel, all aglow. His heart caught in his throat.

One stride and he was back, taking her into his arms, taking her mouth, taking her breath away. He hadn't meant to do it. He knew he shouldn't do it. But for this one moment, he had to do it.

He filled her mouth and took her sweetness as though he'd been starving for it. Her response was without indecision, so clear and pure and full of affection, it made him tremble.

Pulling her body close, into the curve of his chest, of his hips, he knew she must feel how he wanted her. He needed her to feel it. She had to know he wasn't going to hesitate tomorrow night. He ached to take her body the way he'd taken her mouth. He was more than ready—all flesh and blood and urgency.

Wasn't that the point of all this?

Pulling away, he took her face between his hands and looked deeply into her warm dark eyes.

"Thank you, Callie," he said in a low, hoarse voice. "You make my dreams come true."

Turning, he went quickly into the night.

CHAPTER SEVEN

THE ranch was completely decorated for a wedding. *Her* wedding. Callie was astounded.

"I can't believe it. Look at this place!"

Hanging baskets dripping with flowers hung all along the overhang. Someone had put up a tiny picket fence along the walkway to the house and planted vines with white flowers to wind through the slats. Roses were everywhere—in planters, in bowls, in cones set at the corners.

And inside, the decor was even more elaborate.

"Rosa, everything is so beautiful!" Callie cried as the housekeeper let them in.

"Of course," Rosa said, shrugging. "It's a wedding."

Gena came up from behind her and swept Callie away. "Come on up to my room. I've got something to show you."

Callie followed her up the stairs, lugging her overnight case filled with the white suit and accessories she'd brought along. One step into the room and she knew she was probably not going to use it after all. There, on a dressmaker's model, was the most gorgeous white lace and satin gown she'd ever seen.

She gasped. "Oh, it's beautiful!" She got close but didn't dare touch it. "Where did it come from?"

Gena smiled. "It's mine."

Turning, she stared at the woman. "You were married?"

"Almost. The wedding didn't quite come off like I planned." Reaching out, she pulled at the waist. Callie noted a sad look in her eyes, but Gena pushed that away with a sigh and turned back to smile at her. "It'll be a little big for you, but we've got a lady here on the housekeeping staff who's quite a seamstress. She's coming up to take a few tucks, so put it on and we'll see how we're doing."

The next hour was filled with talking and trying on and sewing, and Callie had to admit, she was so relieved. She was actually going to get to wear a wedding dress. Now things were beginning to fall into place and feel right again.

In fact, she got so comfortable, she felt at ease asking Gena a question.

"Tell me about Grant's wife," she said, turning in her chair. Gena was working on Callie's hair, making ringlets to frame her face and weaving tiny seed pearls everywhere.

"His *first* wife, you mean?" Gena corrected with a smile. She thought for a moment before going on. "Jan was like a hummingbird, small and beautiful and always on the move. She was a firecracker of a person, full of opinions and new causes and things that she was driven to get done. She and Grant met in college. They got married right after he graduated."

Callie nodded, glad to have some picture in her mind where there'd been only questions so far.

"So their child wasn't born until quite a while after they married."

"Right." Gena glanced at her, hesitated, then went on. "I don't think Jan actually wanted children. She was too busy. But she finally gave in and did her duty."

Gena frowned thoughtfully, not noticing that Callie was startled by what she'd just said. After all, the Grant she knew was all about having children. That must have created problems of a sort. Unless Grant's need for babies only cropped up afterward.

"They had their ups and downs, but Grant adored her. He was devastated when she was killed in the accident. And losing Lisa, his beloved baby, almost destroyed him. It was months before he could even talk about it. I really thought he would never marry again. It was too deep a wound." She shook her head, pressing her lips together as she thought about it.

"You know, for a long time, he couldn't look at a picture of either one of them. I finally convinced him he had to put a picture up in his office. But you notice where he put it—high up behind his desk at an angle, a place he never looks."

"Then why put it up at all?"

"As a tribute. I went in with him the day he put it up.

I told him he couldn't pretend they had never existed. They deserve more. And he agreed."

Callie shook her head, feeling so sorry for Grant she was afraid her eyes would fill with tears. And with the makeup she and Gena had just put on, that would be a disaster.

"What do you think about what we're doing, Gena?"

She was silent for a moment.

"I'll be honest, Callie. I wasn't for this at the first. But now that I've gotten to know you a little bit, I've changed my mind."

Callie smiled at the woman who would soon be her sister-in-law. "I'm glad. I only hope you're right."

Grant was pacing the floor. Things had definitely gotten out of hand and that meant he wasn't happy. He was a man who liked to have control of every situation he put himself in.

"Why the hell should I put on this monkey suit?" he demanded from Will, who was lounging on the bed and laughing at his friend's hissy fit.

"Because you're going to give that little gal a proper wedding, that's why."

He rounded on his friend, his hands balled into fists. "Says who?"

Will grinned. "Says your sister, Gena."

"Oh."

His older sister was the one person in the world he did take orders from. He ran a hand through his hair distractedly. Maybe he and Callie should reconsider his idea of skipping out on the party and leaving it to the people who wanted it.

"Listen, it wasn't supposed to be this kind of wedding."

"Everybody knows that. Never mind. Go with the flow."

"Going with the flow usually ends up getting you drowned," Grant muttered.

"Not this time. We're going to be there to hold your head above water. That's what this is all about—family and community support."

Grant grimaced. Will was right. And that was exactly why he and Callie were stuck with this thing. They couldn't disappoint their loved ones.

"Never thought I'd see you so nervous," Will commented dryly.

Grant shot him a look. "I'm not nervous."

"The hell you aren't." Will rose from his lounging position and began to unbutton his shirt. "Time to put on my own monkey suit, I guess. Since I'm being forced to stand up for you, seein' as how nobody else will do it. As if I didn't have better things to do with my morning."

"Exactly my point," Grant muttered, preparing to dress for the wedding.

"At least we don't have to get our hair done," Will joked. "Though the way you've been torturing yours, someone better attack it with a comb."

"You come near me with hairdresser intentions and the wedding's off," Grant responded sharply.

Will shrugged good-naturedly. "Never mind. I always did think the windblown look suited you just fine."

Grant held up his hand, listening. Someone was playing the piano downstairs. "They brought in a piano player?"

Will nodded. "And some lady's going to sing, too, from what I hear."

Grant groaned. "This is like a real wedding."

His friend clapped him on the shoulder. "That's the point, big boy. You get the picture. This *is* a real wedding."

But Grant was looking right through him, his mind in turmoil. Somehow this made everything different. How could this be a mere business deal when you added piano players and orange blossoms? How had everything careened so quickly out of control? Callie had been right the night before. This was all a bit too much. But it was obviously too late to change things now.

Coming down the stairs a few minutes later, Grant saw Tina arriving. He'd sent a car for her and was glad to see she'd made it. And then he saw her little girl coming in behind her—the little girl who looked so much like his Lisa that he looked twice to make sure it wasn't her. He had to reach out and take hold of the banister for a moment.

Why was she here? Why would someone bring a little girl like that to a wedding?

He knew it was irrational, but he couldn't help his reaction. When he saw the child, he reacted in an emotional way he couldn't seem to control. The pain swept over him again, intense and almost unendurable. He couldn't have a little girl who looked like Lisa watching as he married Callie. He was usually a logical, unemotional guy, but something about that just struck him as wrong.

He searched for Rosa and pointed out Tina's child. "Could someone watch her during the wedding?" he asked. "Maybe take her up to the old playroom?"

"Of course," Rosa said with a smile. "Such a pretty little girl."

Gena had come up behind him. "What are you doing?" she asked as Rosa hurried off.

Grant avoided her gaze with a guilty maneuver. "Uh, that's Tina's little girl. I thought she would be happier playing away from the wedding."

Gena frowned. "Did Tina ask you to do that?"

"No, but…" He swallowed hard and turned to look his sister in the face. "Look at her. She looks exactly like Lisa. Don't you see? I can't have her here during the wedding. I just can't."

Frowning, Gena stared at the little girl then turned back. "Grant, I don't see…" But he was already heading back up the stairs and he ignored her comment.

There was no way he could explain. Every time he looked at Molly, he saw Lisa and he felt his own little girl looking at him with a sad reproach he just couldn't face. That was all there was to it. And there wasn't much he could do to change that.

Finally it was time. The backyard had been set up with chairs leaving an aisle down the middle. He walked down that aisle behind Will and they took their positions. The place was packed and he had another qualm, hoping Callie didn't feel intimidated.

"What did you do, take an ad out in the local paper?" Will muttered to him out of the corner of his mouth, looking around at the crowd.

"Not me," Grant murmured back. "You can't pin this one on me."

He looked at his grandfather, sitting in the front seat. The old man gave him a smile that helped make up for a lot of this. At least Grant Carver IV was happy.

The pianist struck up "Here Comes the Bride" and Tina came out, looking pleased as punch, and then Callie, looking so beautiful, he could hardly breathe for a moment.

A wave of relief swept over him. She was smiling at him, looking joyful. It was going to be all right. They would get through this and then, tonight, they were going to begin the task of making a beautiful baby together. He was looking forward to that a lot more than he'd expected to. In fact, almost too much.

He settled down and greeted his bride as she reached him.

"Hi," she whispered.

"Hi, gorgeous," he whispered back.

"Let's get married," she said, and he grinned.

"Let's do it."

Magic. That was the only word she could think of for today. Pure, shimmering, golden magic. She'd thought she'd feel awkward with a room full of people she'd never met before. The only people who were really there for her were Tina and Molly and Grant and his sister. But that seemed to be enough, because everyone else acted as though they'd known her since she'd toddled out into the world. She was the center of attention and praise and questions—she'd never felt so in demand before in her life.

Everyone was so happy for her and for Grant, thinking they were on their way to a lifetime of blissful happiness. At first she felt a little strange about pretending this was a normal marriage and not a business deal. She had to admit they'd put on the trappings of a real love match, so why would anyone think any different? But there was no way to explain. No one would understand.

And anyway, she wasn't much different from the others—even she was beginning to feel like this was a love match. Whenever she looked at Grant she couldn't help but react to how handsome he looked in a tuxedo. She felt a quiver inside. Was this the way love began?

That's not love, you ninny! That is just pure anticipation of your wedding night, that's what that is.

Maybe. There was no denying her heart skipped a beat every time she thought of it. So what? It was exciting and it was wonderful and she could hardly wait to be alone with him. She was on pins and needles, but in a good way. A very good way.

And then, Tina had caught the bouquet and the champagne punch bowl had been drained and the finger sandwiches had all been devoured and cake had been smashed into faces and icing licked off fingers and it was time for them to go.

They joined hands and thanked everyone for coming. People were laughing and calling out good wishes. She'd heard someone had tied things to the back of Grant's car. She saw someone passing out little bags of rice.

This was crazy. It was a real wedding. She'd never thought it would happen to her. She turned to look up into Grant's handsome face.

"One kiss," he whispered. "And we're out of here."

She nodded happily. He bent and touched his lips to hers. She sighed. Magic.

And then it all fell to pieces, like a glass vase smashed by a rock.

Someone shouted. A buzz went through the assembly. Callie turned, confused. What was going on?

"Call 911," someone shouted. "Quick. It's Tina."

"Tina?"

Callie was pushing her way through the crowd, her heart in her throat. By the time she got to her friend, Tina was sitting up, supported by someone who was holding a cup of water to her lips.

"I'm okay," she said, trying to smile at Callie. "I'm just…" Her voice faded and she slumped forward.

She wasn't okay at all. That much was obvious. Callie was frantic until the paramedics arrived to take her to the hospital.

"I have to go with her," she told Grant. "I'm so sorry, I…"

He nodded. "Of course. Go."

"I'll call you from the hospital."

"Fine."

He watched her climb into the back of the ambulance in her wedding gown and he knew his wedding night was a lost cause. But that didn't matter. Tina's welfare was all important now. That, and…

"Where's the little girl?" he asked Gena. "I hope she didn't see any of that."

"No. She's asleep on my bed."

Grant nodded and took in a deep breath. "I guess we'd better look into some sort of child care for her."

"Later," Gena said, putting a hand on his arm. "She can stay with me for now."

"Are you sure?"

"Oh, yes. She's adorable. I'll take care of her until we hear more about Tina."

He nodded, looking broodingly at the road that led away from the ranch, the road Callie had disappeared down, and wondering how long it would be before he had her in his arms again.

It had been a week since his wedding, but he didn't have a wife yet. Tina was home from the hospital but things didn't look good. Callie had been staying at the apartment and spending most of her time at the hospital or taking care of Molly. And Grant was on his own.

So here he sat in his darkened apartment, a glass of bourbon and water in his hand, mulling over where things stood. He'd married Callie, but he hadn't made her truly his wife, and he was about to go out of his mind with gloom over it.

He'd seen her every day. He'd gone over and done what he could for Tina and given support to Callie. He'd hired a service of rotating nurses and child-care professionals to help out at the apartment once Tina was back from the hospital. This was a very trying time for all of them.

Callie had decided to stay at the apartment herself for the short-term, and he'd agreed. Even with a nanny hired, he knew she felt someone should be with Molly to keep her from sensing how scary things really were. He wanted Callie home, but he hadn't pushed. He'd had to bite his tongue a number of times to keep from saying what he felt. But he'd held it back.

What was happening to Tina was tragic and heart-breaking. The cancer she'd been battling over the last year had returned with a vengeance. Chemotherapy and radiation were being considered. Callie had thrown herself into the role of support for her friend and he could understand that. Callie's compassionate side was one of the factors that made her such a quality person.

And she was. The better he got to know her, the more impressed he was with the woman he'd chosen to be the mother of his future children. She was great.

And at the same time, she was so much the opposite of his first wife. Jan had been all fire and passion, dancing and laughter, sharp anger and sweet atonement. She'd kept him on his toes. He'd loved her with a passion just as deep and bright, and he missed her so much he avoided thinking about her.

Just because she'd been such a presence in his life, he'd known he needed someone completely different, someone who wasn't like Jan at all. And Callie was that person. Where Jan ran on impulse, Callie was planned. She used logic and kept her distance until she was sure of what she was doing. He was learning to appreciate those qualities more and more.

Now she was coming home tomorrow. And in some ways, he was more worried about that than anything. A bad pattern had been set by their being apart all this time. That pattern had to be broken. He wasn't sure how and he didn't want to come off like a caveman; he only knew something had to give.

He had a strange feeling in the pit of his stomach. Once she came back if she still had that lost, haunted look in her eyes, chances were good she wasn't going to be in the mood for babymaking. He'd promised he wouldn't push her into anything until she was ready. Circumstances were conspiring to keep that from happening. She was going to need something to pull her out of her current sad reality. Something new. Something to jolt her world and make her see the sunshine.

And, what the hell, something to make her see *him* again.

He frowned, turning the glass in his hand, thinking

over options. He had to do something, no matter what it was. What was the point of having a lot of money if you didn't use it?

An idea came to him, full of possibilities. Narrowing his gaze, he thought over all the options hard and fast. Yes. It was a good idea. In fact, it was a fantastic idea.

He picked up the telephone and punched in the number of the local airport. He was going to order himself up a honeymoon.

CHAPTER EIGHT

CALLIE had barely walked in the door when Grant was hustling her back out it again. In minutes, he had her ensconced in his car and they were sailing along the highway toward the airport.

"Where are we going?" she asked, looking out the window at the passing scene. He'd astonished her and she realized she was glad. With so much sadness in her life right now, she needed a respite. She'd spent so many nights lying awake in anger at what was happening to Tina. She'd spent hours crying in the shower, away from Molly. Grief was exhausting. She needed a break.

"It's a surprise."

She frowned. "But I didn't pack anything. Are we staying overnight?"

He smiled mysteriously and refused to answer.

"You see, this is the problem with surprises," she fretted, only half teasing. "Women need to prepare for these things. We need time to decide what to wear."

"I'll keep that in mind for next time," he said smoothly, ignoring her mock glare.

He could have told her not to worry. It had already been taken care of. He'd called the personal shopper at the island resort where they were staying. He'd given her a few sizes and colors to work with and if she did her job well, a whole weekend wardrobe should be waiting for Callie in their room.

They landed on Santa Talia, a little-known island in the Caribbean. The air felt like liquid silk and smelled like plumeria blossoms. The locals had borrowed a tradition from the Hawaiians and happily piled flower leis around both their necks, until they were swimming in perfume and petals.

The resort consisted of bungalows spread out across rolling greenery and centered around a main building that provided the lobby, dining room and shops. Callie exclaimed over the perfectly furnished room and then gasped when she found the closet full of clothes that were just her size.

"I feel like Cinderella," she told him, happily flinging clothes on the bed to look at them.

"Just call me the Handsome Prince," he teased. "But hang on to those glass slippers."

She laughed but when he caught her eye, she blushed. She knew why they were here. She could feel his growing excitement. She was ready, but completely panicked at the same time.

The last week had been draining and the sadness and

anger over what was happening to Tina still filled her with an uncontrollable need to do something, anything, to feel like she was helping. So it had taken a lot for her to leave the scene, and when she'd first realized they were flying off somewhere for the weekend, she'd silently rebelled for a moment or two.

But she realized she owed Grant something, too. And if a few hours away from Texas would help him, maybe they were just what she needed as well.

"Let's go for a walk on the beach," he suggested.

"Okay."

The sun was setting. They hadn't eaten but neither one of them was hungry. They strolled down the white sand, letting the water lap at their toes, then climbed on some rocks. Grant caught hold of her when she lost her footing. He held her against him for a beat longer than necessary. She could feel his pulse, sense his desire. And for a moment, she could hardly breathe.

They had a sumptuous dinner served in their room but she could hardly eat a bite. A bottle of champagne was provided and they drank a toast.

"To honeymoons," Grant said, lifting his glass until the tiny bubbles sparkled in the lamplight.

"To honeymoons," she agreed, smiling into his eyes.

They went for another walk along the sand. The sky was inky and the moon was a silver ship riding the clouds above them. Moonlight shimmered on the water. The refuge of their room looked inviting as they returned. And Grant very deliberately closed the door.

Cupping her face with his hands, he bent slowly toward her and touched her lips with his.

"I promised you we wouldn't do this until you're ready," he said softly. "Are you ready?"

She nodded, her throat too thick for speech. Her heart was like a caged bird fighting against the bars. She'd never been so scared and so thrilled, all at once. She wasn't sure she was going to live through this. But she was ready.

He muttered something against her lips, but she wasn't sure what it was, and then he was parting them with his tongue. She accepted him into her mouth, at first hesitant, and then greedily. He tasted so good and felt amazing. Raising her arms to circle his neck, she arched into his muscular body, wanting to feel her breasts hard against his chest.

Music was playing somewhere nearby. The sound of the waves on the beach mixed with the tune and made an island symphony. The air was soft, his hands were just rough enough to tantalize, and a fire was beginning to smolder inside her in places she didn't know could burn.

His hands slid down her sides and then the simple dress she'd worn was in a puddle on the floor. She heard someone moan and realized the sound had come from her own mouth. She was going to make love and be made love to for the first time in her life. That was just awesome. A landmark. A red-letter day.

Would she be glad or sorry when it was over? She didn't know. She only knew it had to be done. And now her body was reaffirming that very mandate. She was melting and yet floating at the same time. She didn't feel normal at all, and she loved it. As she pressed her mouth to his neck and kissed him with her tongue, she knew she could get addicted to this feeling. And then, suddenly, she felt an urgency building inside her, a need so intense, she cried out in surprise.

"Just a moment, Callie," he whispered huskily against her throat. "Don't worry. We'll get there."

As he picked her up to carry her to the bed, she knew she was sinking into passion as though it were a very thick and very soft pillow. And passion was a destination she never wanted to leave again.

Sometime later, they lay together, spent for the moment, catching breaths. A whole new world of sensation had opened up for Callie, but there was more. A whole new world of closeness and affection had opened up as well. She knew what it was to have a man. Did she also know what it was to love?

She would have said yes to that question just moments before. Now that the air was cooling her skin, she wasn't so sure anymore.

"Cooler heads prevail," she murmured groggily.

"What's that?" he asked, raising his head and looking at her with a slight smile.

"Nothing. I'm just enjoying the moment," she said, smiling at him. She reached a lazy hand up to touch the skin of his wonderful chest. "I feel so…so good."

"I'm glad." He looked at her warmly, and then almost imperceptibly, his gaze cooled. He looked away. "I hope that did us some good," he said crisply, sounding like things were all business again. "We'll have to keep trying until…"

She closed her eyes, appalled, and drew back her hand. Here she'd been thinking love and he'd revealed he had a calculator where his heart should be. For just a moment, she understood the old saying that hatred is the closest thing to love.

Oh, Grant, don't ruin this.

He leaned over her and began dropping small kisses around her navel. To her shock, her hunger was back so strongly, it was as though it hadn't been satisfied just moments before.

So this was the way it was going to be. Alternating joy and chagrin. Well, if that was her destiny, bring it on. She had to admit, she rather liked it.

By the time their honeymoon ended, they'd had two days of mostly bliss. Callie didn't think she'd ever been so happy in her life. She was an old hand at making love now. She knew the ropes. A lady with experience. That made her laugh at herself, but it was true. They'd made love three times that first night and countless times since. And each time she felt she learned a little more about this man she'd married.

For the short time they were together on the island, they developed a closeness that amazed her. He'd been so warm and loving, she felt as though she could say anything to him, and ask anything of him. Well, almost anything. As long as it had nothing to do with his first wife and child.

And now they were going home. Already missing the place, she looked about to make sure they had picked everything up before leaving.

"Have you had a good time?" Grant asked, smiling at her.

"Oh, it's been like heaven here," she said.

"Heaven I'm not so sure about," he responded with a grin. "But I do agree it's about the best place on our earth." He looked at his watch. "We all packed and ready to go?"

"I think so."

"We've got about twelve minutes before the car arrives to take us to the airport." He looked at her speculatively. "Twelve whole minutes," he said softly.

She started to smile, eyes sparkling. "Twelve whole minutes, huh?"

He nodded, one eyebrow quirked in question. "What do you think?"

She shrugged, feeling an unfamiliar sense of wicked delight. "Why not?"

Laughing, they began a race to see who would be first getting rid of the clothes they'd just put on. In half a moment, they were back on the bed, tumbling together, hot skin and willing flesh, a heady recipe for ecstasy.

Callie marveled later, when she was remembering this crazy, wonderful event, that her response had become so quick and ready in such a short time. She was very much afraid that it was mostly due to the fact that she loved the man. And, almost as important, she loved his lovemaking.

They were back and it was like stepping out of a beautiful fantasyland into the cold, hard reality of everyday life. Things that had seemed so easy on Santa Talia suddenly seemed impossible to achieve.

It had been late in the evening when they'd driven in from the airport. Callie had gone straight to the kitchen to begin to find her way around and get used to the place. She'd come over a couple of times in the days before the wedding, fixing up the spare bedroom into a retreat of her own and moving some of her things in. He'd wondered why she felt she needed her own space at the time, but he hadn't said a thing. He wasn't sure, really, how he was going to feel when the time came.

She made them both some hot chocolate and they sat at the kitchen table and sipped, talking softly about their weekend. They had both been yawning and he was thinking it was time to go to bed when she'd rinsed out their cups, turned to smile at him. "Well, good night," she said.

And off she went down the hall before he realized what was happening, straight into the spare bedroom. The door closed with a crisp finality. And he was still sitting at the table with his mouth hanging open.

He supposed she was just as tired as he was, but

still… He hadn't realized she was going to value her privacy quite so completely and now he was feeling a bit disgruntled—even a little confused. He'd looked forward to having Callie in his bed, to holding her close in the night. He hadn't had that warm companionship for so long, not since…

Well, Jan of course. Not since Jan.

Funny that he hadn't realized where that thought was going until it got there. Usually Jan was right up-front, foremost in his consciousness. But never mind, he was just tired. This had nothing to do with Callie and the fact that they had made love. Not at all.

His instinct was to go straight to her and bang on the door, asking her just what the hell she thought she was doing. But he controlled the impulse. He'd vowed to treat her more calmly than he used to treat Jan. Give her some space. Let things develop naturally.

Still, he hoped he wasn't going to have to point out to her that one weekend in the Caribbean wasn't necessarily going to be enough to start a long line of descendants hatching. It might take a bit more work. In fact, it was going to take more no matter what.

Callie was leaning against the bedroom door with her eyes closed, listening intently. She'd taken that long, lonely walk down the hall, waiting to hear his voice calling her back, losing hope with every step.

Why didn't he call her? Why didn't he laugh and say, "No, darling, I want you in my bed—all night long."

But he never said a word. She supposed he didn't want her to try to take Jan's place in his bed, so she wasn't going to try to push her way in. She knew that in his mind, Jan was his real wife. Callie was his business partner in this baby-making enterprise. She wouldn't encroach. She wouldn't try to take any more of him than she was due. But it was going to be a cold, lonely night with only memories of Santa Talia to warm her.

Tina was worse. The doctors had decided her cancer was inoperable. Her outlook was not good and that cast a pall over everything.

Callie threw herself back into caretaking with a vengeance. Though she insisted on working a full day at the office, she vowed to spend every moment she could with Tina and Molly, trying to help smooth the transition for them both. The golden idyllic space and time on Santa Talia very quickly began to seem like a dream that had taken place far, far away in a past that was receding.

At dinner that night, Grant was edgy, and she wasn't exactly calm herself. They both knew a moment of truth was coming.

Grant had worked late at the office and Callie had spent a couple of hours with Tina and Molly, after which she'd picked up a nice chicken dinner at the deli. She was arranging it on plates while Grant put together a salad and hunted for dressing in the refrigerator.

They ate slowly, talking about a project the company

was bidding on, avoiding the tragic topic of Tina and what could be done. At one point, Callie yawned.

"You're working too hard," Grant told her. "And you're not getting enough sleep."

"You're right," she admitted. "But I just have so much I need to get done."

"You know, you could leave work early so you'd have more time with Tina," he said a bit gruffly.

She hesitated. "I've thought about that, but it wouldn't really be fair to my co-workers."

He frowned at her. "Callie, this is a special case and it's only temporary. Take the time off. Tina needs you."

She smiled at him, appreciating his thoughtfulness, though she knew full well the unspoken motive had something to do with the fact that he didn't want her to neglect *him,* either. But that was all right. She could understand that.

"Actually Molly needs me most," she said, and his eyes darkened. He looked away as he always did when Molly was the subject. That bothered her, but she didn't have a chance to ask him about it as he was already talking about changes he was making at the office, and about how he was going to have a few extended business trips coming up.

They cleared away the dishes and sat, drinking coffee and talking for a half hour. Callie was beginning to wonder how they were going to manage bedtime tonight, when Grant took the bull by the horns and did it his way.

"Callie," he said, looking at her forthrightly. "Don't you think we ought to get back to work?"

She was startled for a moment. She'd just risen, thinking to go to the sink to rinse out her cup, but she turned back to face him. "You mean…?"

"Yes," he said, rising himself and looking down at her. "That's what I mean."

She searched his eyes. "Are you sure?"

"About what?"

She took a deep breath. "I didn't know if you really wanted me to."

"Callie, look at me. I want you. Don't ever doubt it. I should have a sign painted on my forehead, I Want Callie."

She smiled, wondering how he could say that. "Are you sure?"

"I'm sure."

She shrugged, putting down her cup. "Well, okay then. My bedroom or yours?"

He'd had enough of this. Growling, he picked her up and slung her over his shoulder.

"I'll show you where you belong," he said.

She shrieked and laughed as he carried her into his room and dropped her in the middle of his bed. She was still laughing as he slipped off her blouse and pushed aside her bra. But when his lips touched the pink tip of her breast all laughter faded away and she melted into the passionate woman she'd learned how to be on a Caribbean island.

An hour later, with the lights off and the house

buttoned down for the night, Grant felt calm and fulfilled for the first time that day. He liked the smell of her hair and the feel of her soft skin. He loved to feel her legs wrap around his hips and to feel her fingers dig into his shoulder. He was crazy about the way she cried out when it got really good and he was addicted to the way he felt when their time together came to its high point.

For just a moment the traitorous thought came into his head—Jan never cared all that much for lovemaking. Callie seemed to thrive on it. But he banished that thought quickly. No comparisons. It wasn't right and it wasn't fair.

Still, he felt fulfilled and satisfied, like a lazy cat in the sun, just being with Callie. After they made love, he thought it was so full and sweet and solid that she wouldn't possibly want to leave him. And then he felt her slip out of the bed and pull on her robe. He lay very still with his eyes closed as she walked quietly across the hallway—away from him.

Why didn't she want to stay with him? Her absence left a big, cold, empty place in his bed. It was something he was going to have to do something about.

Lately nights were good, Callie had to admit.

Days were bad. Being cheerful for Tina was getting more and more difficult. She was on pain medication around the clock now and usually asleep. A hospice nurse came by twice a day, and of course, there was the nursing service Grant had hired for her.

Molly had a nanny twenty-four hours a day, but she didn't understand why her mommy was always in bed. Callie tried to be there as often as she could to keep things as normal as possible for the child. That was what was most important.

It was impossible for a child so young to understand what was happening, but she had to sense that something sad was going on. Callie hated that, knowing it must be scary for her. She understood feeling scared of things you were too young to fully comprehend. She'd spent her own childhood often frightened of her mother's drunk boyfriends. She didn't want Molly to have those kinds of memories. At all costs, she had to be protected.

There was one puzzle that still bothered her. Grant had been so generous, hiring the nurse and the nanny and coming by to see Tina every few days. So why did he act so strangely around Molly? He always avoided her. And the sad thing was, the girl was fascinated by him. She lit up like a Christmas tree every time she caught sight of him. It was a nagging problem that didn't show any signs of getting better.

Finally one day she brought it up to his sister.

"Gena, what is it? Why doesn't Grant like Molly?"

Gena had looked pained. She'd dropped by to see her brother, but he was working very late, so she'd stayed to have a chat with Callie instead.

"Is he still acting that way?"

"Yes. He avoids her like the plague."

She nodded, pursing her lips. "He should have talked to you about this himself, but since he hasn't, I'll tell you. He thinks that Molly looks just like his daughter, Lisa."

Callie frowned, trying to think back and picture the photograph he had in his office. "Well, they both have dark hair and dark eyes, but other than that…" She shrugged.

"Exactly. They don't look alike at all. I don't know how he got it in his brain, but now he can't seem to shake it loose. He fixates on it. And that makes it impossible for him to accept her."

"But he has to accept her." She looked at Gena helplessly. "She's going to be mine. For keeps."

Gena's eyes widened. "You mean to tell me you plan to adopt her once Tina is gone?"

Callie nodded, feeling a bit lost. "I promised Tina. And even if I hadn't…"

Gena nodded. "Sure, I understand." With a sigh, she threw her arms around Callie and hugged her tight. "Oh boy," she said. "I'm afraid you and Grant are in for one rocky ride."

"If only I could think of some way to make him look at Molly differently."

Gena drew back and searched her face. "Don't you get it? It has very little to do with Molly. It's all about him. He's feeling guilty. He can't shake the fact that he should have been home more and taken a more active part in his daughter's life. All this moping about is because he can't expunge his sense of guilt."

Callie shook her head. This was the first she'd heard of anything like this. "What are you talking about?"

Gena shook her head. "Grant was the typical workaholic. He lived for business. And Jan wasn't any better. She was so busy with her activities and her girlfriends. The two of them had a nanny for Lisa. There were times when they would work all day, then meet for dinner out, then get home too late to see Lisa that day. Believe me, that wasn't unusual. They were the ultimate yuppie couple, living the modern life and treating their daughter like a pet."

Callie was shocked. Somehow she couldn't imagine Grant letting that happen, no matter how crazy he was about his wife. "So you're saying Grant feels guilty about neglecting Lisa, so he wants to neglect Molly?"

"Now that's putting a bit of spin on it." Gena made a face. "I don't think Grant is actually all that complicated. No, but I'm saying he does feel guilty. He's haunted by this vision of Lisa watching him, crying, wanting more attention, and him just taking off for work instead of giving it to her."

Callie nodded, finally feeling she was getting the picture. It did fit, now that she thought about it. And at some point, when she felt comfortable enough to do it, she was going to bring it up to him and challenge him to change his ways. Just not right now.

Grant seemed to have a strange way of dealing with his grief. Besides the way he acted with Molly, there was the fact that there were no pictures of his first family here in his apartment. She'd searched every room. There wasn't a sign that he'd ever been married before and had a child. And yet, Jan's presence hung over the place and haunted the hallways. She wondered if she would ever get used to that.

But all in all, her relationship with Grant was good and just seemed to get better and better. She enjoyed her work. It was odd having Grant as a boss when she also had his ring on her hand. She knew everyone else was gossiping about it behind her back. She didn't mind. If it gave them entertainment, let them speculate. She was just concentrating on doing a good job and doing the best she could for Tina and Molly at the same time. And, of course, getting pregnant.

Was that ever going to happen? It had been over a month now and still nothing. She was beginning to worry. What if their happy ending was out to lunch?

"Don't worry," Gena told her. "Just relax and let nature take its course. You're not a teenager, you know. Your body is used to its barren state. It's going to have to jog itself into a new mode of being and that might take it a little time. It could happen at any moment now."

Gena was prophetic—and Callie was pregnant, and probably had been when they were talking about it. The little stick in the pregnancy test told the tale.

But by the time she'd done the test, she'd known for over a week. Her swollen breasts had given her the first clue. And then it was as though she could feel her body adjusting to the presence of new, growing life inside her. She felt as though her pelvic bones were loosening, getting ready to accommodate seven or eight pounds of bouncing baby boy or girl. Her skin felt more sensitive. And her stomach felt queasy.

It was all very exciting and wonderful and she wished she could share it with Grant. But she didn't want to tell him just yet. Despite the fact that this was exactly what he was waiting for, she didn't know how he would react. After all, if she told him she was pregnant, would he withdraw? Would his work become more important than she was? And most of all, would he quit wanting to make love with her?

She didn't want that. It made her face burn to admit it, but she loved how he loved her. His rough hands on her soft skin, the feel of his hard, exciting body, the thrust, the cry, the almost animal-like intensity of the need for him, the incredible climax, and then it all dissolved into a tangle of arms and legs and hot, sweet skin and she could close her eyes and rest on his chest and pretend that he loved her. That time of the night was the best time for her. She'd never known this kind of body hunger could even exist. She didn't want it to end.

She kept remembering what he'd said that first time in Santa Talia.

I hope that did us some good... We'll have to keep trying...

She knew him so much better now and she could tell that he had a sort of affection of some kind for her. And she thought it was pretty obvious he liked making love. But if he had this guilt thing going about Lisa, might he not have something similar about Jan? What if he decided he couldn't justify making love with someone who wasn't Jan now that there was no need for it?

That night, lying with him in his bed, she knew she wasn't being fair to him. She listened to his even breathing. He was a good man. He deserved to know. It was only right she should tell him. She would do it the next night, she decided, as she slipped out of his bed and made her way back to her own room.

That put her on pins and needles for most of the day. She got home a little early and fixed a special dinner and set the table with candlelight. And then she waited.

When he finally came in, he barely looked at her and was clearly distracted.

"I've got a business trip," he told her. "Sorry it's so sudden. I've got to go to Madrid. Negotiations on the property acquisitions are falling apart and I've got to go see if I can put Humpty Dumpty together again. I may be gone for more than two weeks."

"What?"

"I'm sorry, Callie. I know it's a bad time. But there's no choice. I have to go."

Reaching out, he drew her close and kissed her lips. That almost made up for the news he'd just given her, because he never made spontaneous gestures of affection like that. She was thrilled and happy for the rest of the evening.

But she didn't tell him her own news. She decided that would have to wait until he was back from Europe. Knowing that the child he yearned for was actually on the way might make it that much harder for him to leave, and this trip was obviously important to him.

No, she would wait. She held her secret close inside and enjoyed thinking about how happy he was going to be when she finally told him.

CHAPTER NINE

TINA died peacefully early on a Monday morning. Callie was by her side. She didn't cry. She had already cried buckets over the last few weeks and she had to maintain a cheerful front for Molly.

Luckily Molly didn't notice that much was different. She hadn't seen her mother much except for quick visits to the hospital for weeks and then asleep from the doorway once she was home. She was getting used to life with Callie and Nadine, the nanny Grant had hired, filling the caretaking slots. So it didn't seem odd to her when she and Callie packed up all her things to move her to the penthouse. It was just another adventure.

The funeral was on Thursday. It was sparsely attended. Tina didn't have a wide circle of friends. Gena came and Callie appreciated that. Grant tried to make it, taking a midnight flight from Madrid, but his plane was delayed and he only arrived for the tail end of the service. Callie took one look at him coming in through

the arched doorway and all the emotion she'd held so
tightly controlled let go as though a dam had been
broken. She dissolved into tears and he reached her
quickly, taking her into his arms and holding her tightly
against his chest, rocking her and murmuring comfort.
She couldn't seem to stop crying but she loved the way
he held her.

She regained control as they drove back to his apartment. By the time they were at the front door, she was
herself again, quietly telling Grant about how the last
few days had gone. He listened sympathetically as he
pushed the button to open the door. They both entered,
lingering in the entryway, and suddenly a youthful
screech filled the air as Molly came hurtling toward
them on her little chubby legs.

"What the…?"

Grant turned toward Callie, astounded.

Callie caught Molly up in her arms and hugged her
tightly. She'd agonized over whether or not to take her
to the funeral, but in the end, she'd decided not to. She
was just too young to deal with whatever hints she might
have picked up on as to what the ceremony was about.
So she'd left her at home with Nadine.

"Hello, pumpkin," she said to her now. "Were you a
good girl while we were gone?"

"She was just fine," Nadine said, walking toward
them with her awkward walk and warm, generous
manner. "Did you have a good trip, Mr. Carver?"

Grant was still in shock from finding Molly ensconced in his home. Callie saw it in his face and bit her lip, wishing she'd warned him. But it was too late now.

He muttered something in response to the nanny, but his gaze was on Callie, and she could see that he wanted answers. She was about to hand Molly back when the little girl lunged toward Grant.

"Da Da!" she cried, using the name she'd been using for him from the first. Her face was filled with delight and her little arms stretched toward him.

It took both Callie and Nadine wrestling with the child to get her back under control and out of the room. When Callie came back, Grant was waiting for her, his eyes ice-cold.

"What is Molly doing here?" he asked softly.

Callie sighed. She felt as though she were wilting. After the funeral and everything else from the week, she didn't have much in reserve for arguing. Turning, she looked him straight in the face.

"I was hoping I would come up with a good way to tell you about this, but I just haven't had the time to think about it. I'm just going to give you the facts."

"That would be best."

Callie reached out to steady herself against the high back of a chair. "She's here. She's going to stay with us from now on."

He looked as though he'd been shot.

"Grant, I know how you react to her but I'm sure that will fade quickly if you just let it…"

"No." He was shaking his head emphatically. "No, it's impossible."

She turned her head, avoiding his eyes.

"Callie, it's impossible. I can't have her here. I just can't do it."

She took a deep breath. "Grant, I really think you should try to get over that."

"Get over it?" He stared at her. "How do you get over having your life torn apart? How do you get over losing a child?"

She turned back to face him. "But, Grant, this is another child. A child who needs us. Wouldn't redeeming the life of another child make up at least in part for what was lost?"

His face was cold and his jaw looked like granite. "No."

"I know it was awful. It's still awful." She was pleading now. "But life goes on and you can't take it out on a baby."

He frowned as though he couldn't believe she could be saying these things. "I'm not taking anything out on a baby. I'm just telling you what I can't do. And I can't live with the situation you suggest. I just can't." He sighed impatiently. "Surely Tina has some family somewhere who can take the baby."

She shook her head, fighting the awful feeling of dread that was building in her.

"Oh, come on, Callie. Everyone's got someone."

"I don't. Except you."

She said the last two words so softly he might not have heard. He certainly didn't react.

"And you want me to believe Tina didn't, either?" he said levelly. "She couldn't have been completely alone in the world."

"Well, she does have a stepmother somewhere. But she hated her. Called her evil. I know they haven't spoken in years."

"Still, if she's family…"

She met his gaze with her chin high. "The woman let Tina be sent to foster care rather than take care of her after her father died. Why would she want to take Tina's baby in?"

She saw the hope fade in his eyes, but then he had an idea.

"Then how about some nice young couple looking to adopt? She's a beautiful little girl. She wouldn't have any trouble finding someone who wanted her."

Callie's jaw stuck out even further. "She already has found someone. Me."

"Oh, Callie." He shook his head in disbelief.

She was fighting tears now, but she was determined not to let them show. "Grant, this is Molly we're talking about. My Molly."

"*Your* Molly?"

"Yes." She nodded. "Tina did some paperwork and got me named as legal guardian a week ago. I'm going to adopt her."

His eyes were flat and cold. "Why didn't you tell me?"

She shook her head. "You weren't here."

He stared at her. There was no give in his face, no sign that he might relent. Her heart was breaking.

"I hate to put it this way, Grant, but my responsibility to Molly goes back further than my commitment to you. I can't abandon her. I won't."

He stared at her, hardly able to believe this was the same loving woman he'd become so accustomed to these last few weeks. Where had this steely determination come from?

"There's no one else to take her," she was saying insistently. Her emotions were starting to show. Her voice was rising. "If this means it's over between you and me, that's the way it will have to be, because there is no way I can do that to this child."

Looking at her, he saw the tragedy in her eyes and he realized what she was asking. Could he give her up? Why not? He could find another woman, couldn't he? It couldn't be that hard.

And suddenly, it struck him like a knife in the chest. He couldn't do it. He was so attached to her now, he couldn't imagine life without her. He had to have her nearby. His breath was coming faster than normal and he realized that the threat of Callie leaving scared the hell out of him. He couldn't lose her. He would do just about anything to keep her. But could he do this?

Blinking rapidly, he tried to shift gears, tried to rethink things. Molly was a sweet little girl. It wasn't her fault she affected him the way she did. Maybe… But no. Just thinking about it made him start to sweat. He couldn't do it.

Surely there was someone out there in the world who could take her. Surely there was an aunt, a grandmother, someone. All they had to do was find that person. He had a very good detective agency he used at times for the company. He would call them in the morning. Surely they could find someone.

In the meantime, maybe he could deal with this new situation. He would have to. He couldn't let Callie go. That was not an option.

But the words were difficult to speak.

"We could try it for a while, I suppose," he said, his voice rough as sandpaper. Looking at the hopeful light in her eyes, he wanted to take her in his arms and hold her tightly to him. "We'll see how it goes."

He could see the relief in her face and it warmed him.

"So you want me to stay," she said.

He grimaced. "Of course I want you to stay," he said roughly, trying to control the emotion in his voice.

She sighed and let herself begin to relax. "Well, that's good. Because…because I really should be here right after Christmas." She tried to smile but she knew she looked like she was about to cry. "That's when our baby is going to be born."

"What?" He felt the room spin. It was his turn to reach for support. "You're pregnant?"

She nodded, tears welling in her eyes as she smiled up at him. "Yes."

"Callie." He pulled her close and rained kisses on her face. "Oh, Callie. I'm the happiest man in the world."

And for the moment, he actually meant it.

An almost comfortable routine grew up around their busy days. Callie and Grant ate breakfast together in the mornings, then Grant left for the office and Callie fed Molly and played with her until it was time for her to go to work. She took care of errands and shopping late in the afternoon. Then she went straight home to take care of Molly for the rest of the day into the evening. Grant usually didn't come home until after Molly's bedtime. It was best that way, she supposed.

Still, the situation wasn't ideal and Callie wished Grant would make an effort to get to know Molly better. But she wasn't in the position to be choosy right now. So she let it go for the present.

Her fear that Grant might not feel the need to pay much attention to her once she was pregnant, as though that project had been completed and it was time to move on, proved unjustified. Most of the time their relationship could have passed for a love-match to any casual observer—especially in the lovemaking department. Contrary to her fears, there had been no slacking off in that area. In fact, Grant seemed to relish her changing body, and she relished his interest.

Her pregnancy was progressing normally. Grant insisted on going with her to her first doctor's appointment. The doctor pronounced her in great shape and

Grant talked vitamins and danger signs he'd read about in the waiting room all the way home.

That meant he was home earlier than usual—early enough to witness Molly eating her dinner. The little girl was in her high chair and Callie had turned to the sink to wash off a toy when Grant walked into the room.

"Look at this mess!"

She whirled to see what was going on. "What are you shouting about?"

"There's food all over the white rug." He pointed down. "Look, it's ruined."

She looked at the fancy and probably very expensive carpet and then she looked at Molly. Molly was grinning happily. As Callie watched, she picked up a handful of mashed potatoes and threw it at Grant. The little splat landed on the side of his nose. Molly gurgled happily. Callie could almost hear her saying, "Touchdown!"

Grant turned toward Callie with a see-what-she-did look on his face.

And Callie responded cheerfully with, "Okay. That does it. We're getting rid of the white rug."

Grant looked confused as he wiped mashed potatoes from his face. "What?"

She shrugged. "The white rug has to go. Do you think Molly is the only baby who's going to throw food all over it? White rugs are not compatible with happy babies."

"But…"

"You just wait." She pointed to her still-tiny tummy. "This guy is going to tear this place apart."

He looked a bit nonplussed.

"We're going to have to baby-proof all the rooms," she said.

"Baby-proof my apartment?"

"Didn't you do that for…?"

She stopped. She'd almost said Lisa's name. That was against the unspoken rules. She saw something flicker in his eyes.

But at the same time, she was having second thoughts. This was all wrong. They couldn't dance around this issue the rest of their lives. Lisa had been a real person and deserved to be spoken about like a real person. The way he was treating her, she wasn't real anymore—she was a museum relic wrapped in protective gauze and kept from human view. He must have memories of her that he cherished. Wouldn't it be better if it was possible for him to bring them back out and honor them?

"I'm sure you did a lot of child-proofing once Lisa began to toddle around the room," she said deliberately.

He looked up at her, startled. It was probably the first time he'd ever heard his baby's name out of her mouth. He stared at her for a long moment, then, without saying a word, he turned and left the room.

Well, it looked like that had been a big mistake. But what else could she do? And something had to be done.

She got a red lollipop for Molly. She'd brought over Tina's store of them and put them in a drawer in the kitchen. She still didn't really approve of Molly having them, but she was willing to let her for a while. She had so many new things to learn and new rules to follow. She liked the idea of giving her as many things from her life with Tina as she could, at least for the time being.

But she also had to work on this fixation of Grant's. The next night, she tried a new method.

She and Grant were sitting on the couch, talking quietly just before bed. Suddenly she brought up something she knew he was going to resist.

"I think we should put up a picture of Jan and Lisa."

He froze, staring at her. "What are you talking about?"

"Grant, they were a huge part of your life. You can't block that out and pretend it never happened."

"I don't." His voice sounded like gravel on glass. "Believe me. I think of them every hour of every day."

"Yes, but you think of them in a horrible way. You think of their deaths and how miserable you are without them. You should think about the good times. Maybe if we put up pictures…"

He was shaking his head. "You don't understand at all."

She ignored that. "Let's let the rest of our little family know who they were and that they are still important."

He was scowling blackly. "They're only important to me."

"No. You're wrong. They are a part of who you are. And that's important to me."

He scoffed. "Should we put up a picture of Ralph, too?"

She shook her head. "No. Ralph wasn't really important to anyone but his mother." She smiled, thinking of it. "Funny, but I think his mother was always more important to me than he was."

Which reminded her, a visit to Marge was overdue. It had been two weeks since she'd gone by to see her mother-in-law. It was time to go and tell her about the pregnancy—even though she probably wouldn't understand.

Grant hadn't agreed to let her put up the pictures she wanted to display. She would work on it. Eventually she was sure he would give in. After all, it was to his benefit that he do so. But for tonight, she'd at least pushed a hint of a nose under the tent. And now it was time to start anticipating bedtime—her favorite time of day.

The next night, she had a new angle.

"Could we get a better scanner for the computer?" she asked him. "The one we have here is pretty flaky and I've seen new models that do a much better job on photos."

"What are you scanning?"

"I found a cupboard full of pictures of…of Jan and Lisa. I want to copy them so that…"

"What?" He stared as though he thought she'd gone crazy.

"For scrapbook pages. Have you seen the sort of scrapbooking that everyone is doing these days? That's what I want to do. I want to make a scrapbook filled with the story of your life with your first family. Because the history needs to be preserved and told and not let to drift away."

He didn't look pleased, but he didn't comment, and the next night, she found a new scanner in the entryway.

She fixed up the little office off the kitchen as a scrapbooking room. She had pictures on bulletin boards all around as she tried to work out how she wanted to do her pages and develop a timeline. She started it as a duty but she quickly learned to love doing it. Every evening she tried to go in and spend some time working on her project. On at least two occasions, Grant came to the door and looked in. He didn't say anything. But the second time he stayed, watching her work for a good ten minutes before he turned away.

The next day, she took one of the best pictures she'd found—a studio photo of Jan and Lisa—and had it framed, then put it up in the hallway. When Grant came home that night it was the first thing he saw.

"What the hell is that?" he demanded.

"I think you can see what it is." She tried to remain calm but her heart was beating like a drum.

He turned to glare at her. "If I wanted a picture like that up I'd have put it up," he said.

"This isn't for you, necessarily," she said stoutly. "It's for me. And for the baby that's coming. You don't have to walk by this part of the hallway if you can't stand it. You can walk the other way."

He gazed down at her with his brow furled. "Callie, what the hell are you trying to do?"

"I think you have to try to normalize your feelings. You can't let wounds fester forever."

He slapped the wall with his open hand and barked,

"What right do you have to decide how my wounds should heal?"

She drew breath deep into her lungs and faced him bravely. "For myself, none at all. But I do have a right for our baby."

He stared at her for a long moment, but he shook his head. "No," he said. "Maybe you can make that argument after the baby comes. But you can't make it now." Reaching out, he took down the picture. "Sorry, Callie," he said coolly. "No can do."

He walked off with the picture, but she noticed that he was looking at it. So she'd lost this round. But every time he was forced to talk about his first family, or look at pictures of them, she felt it moved him more toward accepting the past. And maybe she was just kidding herself, but she felt she was making progress. At least she hoped so.

CHAPTER TEN

CALLIE was clearing away the dishes from dinner a few nights later. Grant helped her, then dropped down onto the couch to read the paper. Out of the corner of her eye, Callie could see Molly, who was supposed to be in bed, wending her way into the room, hugging the shadows as though she knew she wasn't really welcome.

Callie turned to get rid of the glasses she was putting away before she could intercept Molly. But the little girl was too fast for her, and by the time she'd turned back, Molly was already at Grant's knee, tugging on his slacks with one sticky hand and holding out a half-eaten red lollipop with the other.

"Da Da!" she cried.

The look on Grant's face would have been comical if the whole situation wasn't so sad.

"Take it," Callie urged softly. "Grant, take it!"

Very reluctantly, he did, grasping the sloppy-looking candy between his thumb and forefinger. "Callie, what the hell am I supposed to do with this?" he growled.

She swept the baby up in her arms and squeezed her tightly. "Grant says 'thank you', Molly. He loves that lollipop." Giving her a loud, wet smack on the cheek, she hurried her back to the nanny's care.

When she got back, he was washing his hands in the sink.

"You do realize she was offering you her most prized possession," she noted dryly. "I guess I'm going to have to teach her that you can't buy love."

"Callie…"

She saw the tortured look in his eyes and regretted her words. "I'm sorry. But she's just a child and she wants you to like her."

"I like her," he said, though his tone was forced. "It's not her fault that she reminds me so much of…"

"Of Lisa," Callie said. She was making a point of talking about them now. "I know. And I know you're trying to be kind to her. You're really making an effort."

"But you want me to love her like she was my own," he said. "And, Callie, that's just not going to happen."

Maybe not. Maybe it was hopeless. And maybe there would come a time when she had to decide who needed her more: Molly or Grant. She only hoped it never came to that, because she wasn't sure which way she would go.

Something woke Grant up the next morning—a movement on the bed beside him. His heart leaped. Had Callie come back to him on her own? He turned and met a pair of dark, laughing eyes, and then a little chubby fist hit him in the cheek and Molly giggled.

"Da Da!"

He jerked back.

"Callie!" he called.

Molly began to bounce on the bed, laughing uproariously.

He turned back to look at her, frowning fiercely. But as he watched, his frown faded. She did look cute. If only he could look at her once and not see Lisa's reproachful face.

"There you are, you rascal," Callie said, coming in and standing at the edge of the bed. "Are you torturing Grant again?"

Molly giggled and bounced out of reach.

"I'll get her out of here," Callie said, reaching for the moving target.

But Grant was smiling at her. "Why don't you come join us instead?" he suggested as he pulled her down on top of him.

"Grant!" She laughed as she slid over to his side. "What are you doing?"

"Enjoying you," he murmured, looking sensual.

"Oh my," she said. "I didn't realize it was open house today."

"I wish I could wake up this way every morning," he said, touching her cheek with his forefinger.

He barely got the words out when Molly dove between them, chattering happily as though she thought she should be part of the conversation.

His head jerked back in surprise and Callie pushed up on her elbow, preparing to make Molly move.

But Grant had calmed himself. "Let her stay," he said. "It's okay."

Callie had to work hard to keep from choking aloud. A happy bubble was rising in her chest.

"She's just being a little dickens this morning," Callie said lovingly. "Nadine tells me that she had to spend half the day yesterday racing around stuffing things back into drawers after Molly emptied them out."

"So she's already getting into the drawers," Grant said. He remembered when Lisa had been at that stage. As he thought of it and pictured Lisa, he steeled himself and waited for the pain to come. But there was nothing. After a moment, he began to wonder why.

They cuddled in the bed for another five minutes and then it was time to get up. But the warm feeling stayed with him all the rest of the day.

Callie was sure they were making progress, but one big hurdle still remained. Gena had said he was racked with guilt. If that was true, surely it would do him good to get it out in the open and talk about it. Did she have the nerve to bring it up?

One night about a week later, he was packing for another business trip. It seemed like a good time. She waited for him to come out of his room, and she told him she wanted to talk about something. He sat down with her on the couch and she launched into it.

He listened to her version of Gena's theory about his feeling guilty because he didn't pay as much attention to Lisa when she was alive as he should have and didn't say a word. Instead he got up and poured himself a drink and went to sit on the balcony, away from her.

She was pretty sure he was furious with her. And why not? Did she really have a right to push him on this?

But an hour later, when he came in, he pulled her into his arms and buried his face in her hair.

"That last day," he said, his voice a bit hoarse, "it was obvious Lisa was coming down with something in the morning. I had a meeting. Jan had a presentation she was giving at Junior League. Neither one of us paid much attention to Lisa. We thought we were so damn busy with such important things."

His voice broke and it was a moment before he could go on.

"The nanny tried to call us all day, but my cell phone wasn't working right and Jan didn't pick up because she was in a meeting hall until late in the afternoon. When she finally got home, Lisa was burning up and the nanny was hysterical. She tried to call me, but the cell still wasn't working and my secretary was out for the afternoon. So she packed Lisa into the car and went racing off to the hospital. She ran a red light. And got hit. She lived another twenty-four hours, but Lisa was killed in the original impact."

"Oh, Grant. Oh, I'm so sorry."

He pulled away and just shook his head.

"But it wasn't your fault. How could you…?"

"Don't patronize me, Callie," he said harshly. "Of course it was my fault. If I'd been a proper father and husband, the accident would never have happened. Of course it was my fault. And I'll pay all the days of my life."

She refused to be cowed by his anger at himself. Following him into his room, she shut the door and made him face her. "You listen to me, Grant Carver," she said sternly. "You are a wonderful, caring man. You may have been careless in the past, but you're older now, more mature. You won't let family needs slide ever again."

"How do you know? What makes you so sure?"

"I know you. I've seen you in action. And most of all…" She walked into his arms. "I love you."

His face registered shock. He hadn't expected that. She was playing against the rules again, coloring outside the lines. He didn't have an answer, but she didn't care. Stepping forward, she rose on her toes and put her arms around his neck.

"Make love to me, Grant," she whispered. "If you can't love me, at least make love to me. That's all you ever promised, and I'm holding you to it."

"I will, Callie," he agreed, cupping her cheek in his hand. "If you promise to stay with me all night. Can you do that?"

She looked up at him, surprised. "Of course. Are you sure you want me to? I thought…well, I know you still consider Jan your real wife and I thought…"

"Oh, Callie." He crushed her in his embrace. *"You're*

my wife. Don't you ever doubt it. I've been aching to have you where I can hold you all night long."

Tears welled in Callie's eyes. "Grant," she whispered. "I'd be honored to share your bed."

He pulled her down onto the velvet comforter and she knew she had a home there at last.

Grant sat down in the plane, ready for his flight to San Francisco, and stared at his briefcase. He had put a large manila envelope inside. Though he hadn't opened the envelope yet, he knew what it contained. The detectives he'd hired were finally giving him a report on all Molly's living relatives. This was what he'd been waiting for. He planned to peruse the document while in his hotel room, but he wasn't looking forward to it.

He had enough to think about for now. For the entire flight, he agonized over all his missteps and misstatements in his recent relationships. He wondered how Callie had put up with him all this time. She was wonderful and he was so lucky to have found her.

When he got to the hotel, he put his bag on the bed, worked the lock and snapped open the case. He began to pull clothes out and very quickly, he noticed something strange. Someone had added something to the clothes he'd packed. The more he dug, the more he found. Red lollipops were stuffed in every crevice of his suitcase. It looked as though a lollipop-loving squirrel had been at work.

And then the coup de grace. The fine wool suit-coat he was planning to wear to a very important meeting had a half-eaten lollipop stuck to the lapel. Stickiness courtesy, he was sure, of little Molly.

He stared at it for a long, long moment. He waited for the anger to explode in his chest and build in his head. But it didn't happen. Instead he started to laugh.

"Molly, Molly," he said, shaking his head. "Oh, Molly."

He laughed until tears filled his eyes.

That night he had a dream and the little dark-haired girl whose face swam into the picture was Molly, not Lisa. And she was smiling.

He woke up and lay staring at the ceiling, thinking. He was on edge, restless. He wanted something. He was aching for someone now, and it wasn't Jan. It was Callie.

Callie. Beautiful, sexy, sensible Callie. What a fool he'd been not to notice.

Rolling out of bed, he went into the bathroom and took a long hot shower, thinking things through. When he came out, he was decided.

He was going home.

The first thing he did was to pull the manila envelope out of his briefcase and tear it to shreds without opening it. Then he called the office where the meeting was to be held and canceled. He lugged his suitcase, lollipops and all, down to the lobby and called for reservations on the next available plane. He was going home to the woman that he loved—and the little girl who thought she could buy love with lollipops.

When he walked into his penthouse apartment, Molly was the first to see him.

"Da Da!" she cried, racing to him.

Pulling the little girl up into his arms, he hugged her. "Thank you for all those lollipops, Molly," he said. "That was a big surprise."

She giggled and was suddenly shy. He hugged her close and kissed her cheek just as Callie walked into the room.

"Grant!" she cried, her face filled with candid joy. "What are you doing here?"

He put Molly down gently and she ran off. Turning to Callie, he shook his head, looking her over from top to toe.

"What's wrong?" she asked, suddenly anxious. "Did I do something?"

"You sure did," he claimed, a slow smile growing on his handsome face. "You made a family for me, Callie. And I didn't even have the intelligence to notice."

She smiled. "Oh, is that all?"

"No. There's something else."

He took her in his arms, looking down with all his love filling his gaze. "You made me love you."

Callie's tiny gasp gave him shivers. "Do you really mean that?" she asked, her dark eyes luminous, "or are you just singing a song?"

"Both," he said. "Will you marry me, Callie?"

"I already did, silly."

"I know. But I just wanted to ask you again."

"Okay. I'll marry you anytime, Grant. Anytime at all."

"Good. Because time is the greatest gift. And I promise, my time will always be yours."

EPILOGUE

MOLLY loved it at the ranch.

She loved the dogs and the horses and the cows. She loved to make the chickens run. She loved finding where the cat had hidden to have her kittens. She loved all the nice people who seemed to love her right back.

But she was sort of scared of Granpa. He sat upstairs in that big chair and growled at her, all his whiskers quivering. Mommy said he was laughing, but it didn't sound like laughing to Molly. He was like the bear in the book Daddy read to her. Scary. And she had to walk past that room to get to the room where the baby was.

The baby!

She knew she was supposed to love the baby, but she wasn't sure yet. She tried to talk to him but he didn't talk much. Not like Molly. Molly was a big girl now. Next week she would be two and she was going to have a big birthday party.

She had been living at the ranch ever since the baby was born with her mommy and daddy—she used to call them Callie and Grant, but those names were too hard to say. Anyway, she liked calling them Mommy and Daddy better.

"Good baby, good baby," she said, patting him on the stomach.

"Don't pat too hard, honey," Mommy said, pulling her hand back.

Molly felt hurt. She wasn't patting too hard. She didn't want to hurt the baby.

"We have to be extra special careful of the baby," Mommy told her, giving her a hug at the same time. "Babies are easy to break. They can get hurt so easily—things we don't even think of can hurt them. So we have to touch very softly."

She nodded. She understood. Babies were precious and special. But she looked up quickly at Callie's face. Did her mommy love the baby better than her?

She didn't have time to find out because Daddy swooped her up in his arms and gave her little baby kisses on the top of her head.

"G'illa, g'illa!" she cried.

"You want gorilla kisses?" he said, laughing at her. "Okay, here goes."

He planted a few loud, rumbling, smacking kisses on her cheeks and her neck and she shrieked with happiness.

"Shh, the baby," Mommy said, and Daddy put her down.

Molly frowned. People said that all the time. "Don't wake the baby, don't wake the baby." The baby was always asleep. What fun was that? Maybe he didn't even know about fun stuff yet.

Daddy was kissing Mommy. Mommy was kissing him back and that made Molly feel warm and happy.

Daddy seemed to feel the same way, because he said, "I never knew a man could be this happy. I bless the day you tried to kill me with your orchid pot."

Mommy laughed and said, "Me, too. Since that day we've gained a marriage, a daughter and now a son."

"Grant Carver the Seventh," Grant said with satisfaction, looking down at the baby. "We done good."

Mommy and Daddy were happy. That was good. She had a vague sense of missing someone. Mommy told her all the time about Tina, who was her first mommy. Tina went to heaven because God needed her up there. But she would see Tina again someday. She loved Tina, too. She remembered her a little bit and Mommy always showed her pictures.

Molly was getting bored. She thought she heard the cat meow, so she slipped out of the room and headed toward the landing.

She held her breath as she started across the open doorway to where Granpa was sleeping in his chair. But then she saw something. She stopped. There, on a shelf right beside him, was a box with a red lollipop sticking out of it.

Her little heart jumped. She remembered red lollipops. She used to love red lollipops, but Mommy said they weren't good for her. She hadn't had a red lollipop for a long time. And now, there was one right there next to Granpa.

But he was scary. What if he woke up? What if he reached out and grabbed her and growled? Her heart was beating very fast. She crept into the room and reached out. There. The lollipop was in her hand. It was different from the ones she used to have, but...

"What have you got there, young'un?"

She gasped and started to run, her heart in her throat. She couldn't stop. If she stopped, he would take it away from her, and she needed it. Running down the hall, she came to the baby's room and dashed inside. Mommy and Daddy were gone, but the baby was awake.

She pulled on the paper around the candy. It came off easily. Then she climbed up on the chair next to the cradle and leaned down. He had big blue eyes and he stared at her very hard.

"Here, baby," she whispered to him. "Here. Eat."

Suddenly someone was yelling. She jerked back, startled. The maid named Ana was calling out and people were running toward the room.

Ana pulled the lollipop from her hand. "No!" she cried. "You can't give that to the baby. No!"

Molly was scared. She wasn't bad. Didn't they understand? She wanted to give the baby something fun. She wanted to give him the thing she had always loved best. But the faces seemed angry.

Then Daddy was there and he pulled her up into

his arms. "You and your red lollipops," he said, holding her close.

"Don't yell at her," Mommy was saying. "She was doing it out of love."

"You can't do it, though," Daddy told her, being very serious. "You can't give things like that to the baby. He's not ready."

Tears were popping out and running down her fat cheeks and her lower lip was trembling.

"You love the baby, don't you?" Daddy said.

Did she? She looked down at where he was watching. And suddenly, she saw something in his big blue eyes. He was her brother. He was hers. Maybe she did love him. She nodded and gave a big sniff.

"Of course you do."

"Tell you what," Mommy said, tousling her hair. "You wait just a second. I have an idea." She reached in and rummaged in the big bag of baby care items she took with her everywhere these days.

"Here." She pulled out a bright red pacifier and showed it to Molly. "What do you think? Do you want to be the one to give it to him when he's ready?"

Molly's eyes lit up and she nodded, smiling through her tears.

"Only when I say it's a good time, okay? But you will be the keeper of the red pacifier. I'm going to trust you."

"And you know what?" Daddy said. "Next week at your birthday party, you're going to have all the red lollipops you can handle. Okay?"

Molly nodded again and threw her little arms around his neck. She was a big girl now. She was learning lots of things. And that was good, because that little baby was going to have a lot to learn from his big sister and she wanted to be ready.

"We love you, Molly," Daddy said.

She nodded. She knew that. She loved them, too. Even the baby.

* * * * *

Silhouette® Romantic Suspense keeps getting hotter!

Turn the page for a sneak preview of
New York Times *bestselling author*
Beverly Barton's latest title f
rom THE PROTECTORS *miniseries.*

HIS ONLY OBSESSION
by Beverly Barton

On sale March 2007 wherever books are sold.

Gwen took a taxi to the Yellow Parrot, and with each passing block she grew more tense. It didn't take a rocket scientist to figure out that this dive was in the worst part of town. Gwen had learned to take care of herself, but the minute she entered the bar, she realized that a smart woman would have brought a gun with her. The interior was hot, smelly and dirty, and the air was so smoky that it looked as if a pea soup fog had settled inside the building. Before she had gone three feet, an old drunk came up to her and asked for money. Sidestepping him, she searched for someone who looked as if he or she might actually work here, someone other than the prostitutes who were trolling for customers.

After fending off a couple of grasping young men and ignoring several vulgar propositions in an odd mixture of Spanish and English, Gwen found the bar. She ordered a beer from the burly, bearded bartender. When he set the beer in front of her, she took the opportunity to speak to him.

"I'm looking for a man. An older American man, in

his seventies. He was probably with a younger woman. This man is my father and—"

"*No hablo inglés.*"

"Oh." He didn't speak English and she didn't speak Spanish. Now what?

While she was considering her options, Gwen noticed a young man in skintight black pants and an open black shirt, easing closer and closer to her as he made his way past the other men at the bar.

Great. That was all she needed—some horny young guy mistaking her for a prostitute.

"*Señorita.*" His voice was softly accented and slightly slurred. His breath smelled of liquor. "You are all alone, *sí?*"

"Please, go away," Gwen said. "I'm not interested."

He laughed, as if he found her attitude amusing. "Then it is for me to make you interested. I am Marco. And you are…?"

"Leaving," Gwen said.

She realized it had been a mistake to come here alone tonight. Any effort to unearth information about her father in a place like this was probably pointless. She would do better to come back tomorrow and try to speak to the owner. But when she tried to move past her ardent young suitor, he reached out and grabbed her arm. She tensed.

Looking him right in the eyes, she told him, "Let go of me. Right now."

"But you cannot leave. The night is young."

Gwen tugged on her arm, trying to break free. He tightened his hold, his fingers biting into her flesh. With her heart beating rapidly as her basic fight-or-flight instinct kicked in, she glared at the man.

"I'm going to ask you one more time to let me go."

Grinning smugly, he grabbed her other arm, holding her in place.

Suddenly, seemingly from out of nowhere, a big hand clamped down on Marco's shoulder, jerked him back and spun him around. Suddenly free, Gwen swayed slightly but managed to retain her balance as she watched in amazement as a tall, lanky man in jeans and cowboy boots shoved her would-be suitor up against the bar.

"I believe the lady asked you real nice to let her go," the man said, in a deep Texas drawl. "Where I come from, a gentleman respects a lady's wishes."

Marco grumbled something unintelligible in Spanish. Probably cursing, Gwen thought. Or maybe praying. If she were Marco, she would be praying that the big, rugged American wouldn't beat her to a pulp.

Apparently Marco was not as smart as she was. When the Texan released him, he came at her rescuer, obviously intending to fight him. The Texan took Marco out with two swift punches, sending the younger man to the floor. Gwen glanced down at where Marco lay sprawled flat on his back, unconscious.

Her hero turned to her. "Ma'am, are you all right?"

She nodded. The man was about six-two, with a sun-burned tan, sun-streaked brown hair and azure-blue eyes.

"What's a lady like you doing in a place like this?" he asked.

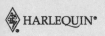

Save $1.⁰⁰ off

**the purchase of
any Harlequin
Everlasting Love novel**

Coupon valid from January 1, 2007
until April 30, 2007.

Valid at retail outlets in the U.S. only.
Limit one coupon per customer.

5 65373 00076 2   (8100) 0 11302

HEUSCPN0407

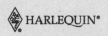

EVERLASTING LOVE™

Every great love has a story to tell™

Fall from Grace

Kristi Gold

Save $1.⁰⁰ off

the purchase of
any Harlequin
Everlasting Love novel

Coupon valid from January 1, 2007
until April 30, 2007.

Valid at retail outlets in Canada only.
Limit one coupon per customer.

52607370

HECDNCPN0407

Hearts racing
Blood pumping
Pulses accelerating

**Falling in love can be
a blur...especially at**
180 mph!

**So if you crave the thrill
of the chase—on and off
the track—you'll love**

SPEED DATING
by Nancy Warren!

Coming Next Month

#3937 CATTLE RANCHER, CONVENIENT WIFE Margaret Way
Outback Marriages

Cattle rancher Rory Compton is looking for a down-to-earth Outback wife. Glamorous fashion editor Allegra Sanders doesn't fit Rory's criteria. With her model looks Rory can't believe his attraction to him is real. But that doesn't stop him from thinking about her—every minute of the day!

#3938 THE MAID AND THE MILLIONAIRE Myrna Mackenzie

Anna Nowell loves her job as maid to wealthy, cultured Donovan Barrett. He was a renowned physician until the tragic death of his son left him grief-stricken. Consorting with the help isn't on his agenda, but Anna's compassion and laughter have a way of changing all his plans.

#3939 BAREFOOT BRIDE Jessica Hart

Alice Gunning loves her job, has a swanky city flat and is about to get engaged. Until one day her boyfriend leaves her, she's fired and her lottery numbers come up! Alice heads for a tropical paradise to work things out, but then she encounters Will Paxman, her gorgeous old flame.

#3940 THE PRINCE AND THE NANNY Cara Colter
By Royal Appointment

Feisty redhead Prudence Winslow has sworn off men. But then she meets Ryan Kaelan and his delightful motherless children. Prudence takes a job as their nanny, telling herself it isn't Ryan's jaw-dropping sexiness that convinced her, or the fact that he is a real-life prince.

#3941 THEIR VERY SPECIAL GIFT Jackie Braun
Heart to Heart

Years of trying for a baby has driven a wedge between Reese Newcastle and her husband, Daniel. Reese has a chance to make her long-cherished dream of motherhood come true by adopting a baby. Could this adorable bundle of joy help them rekindle the magic of their marriage?

#3942 HER PARENTHOOD ASSIGNMENT Fiona Harper

Gaby is a supernanny sent to help families that have hit a brick wall. But the rift between Luke and his daughter can only be healed if Luke allows himself to be healed, as well. In helping to fix this family, Gaby soon realizes her real assignment is to become a mother to Heather...and a wife to Luke!

HRCNM0207